MAGICAL,
FANTASTICAL,
ALPHABETICAL
SOUP

ALSO BY
CHUCK TAYLOR

The One True Cat: A Memoir with Cats

*Saving Sebastian: A Father's Journey through
His Son's Drug Abuse*

Like Li-Po Laughing at the Lonely Moon

Heterosexual: A Love Story

Rips

Poet in Jail

Drifter's Story

Magical, Fantastical, Alphabetical Soup

Mini-Fictions, Prose Poems, and Rants

CHUCK TAYLOR

PINYON PUBLISHING
Montrose, Colorado

Book and Cover Design by Susan E. Elliott

Cover Photograph by Chuck Taylor

Photograph of Lucy In Disguise With Diamonds store in Austin, TX by Chuck Taylor

Photograph of Chuck Taylor by *Insite Magazine* of Bryan, TX

First Edition: July 2013

Pinyon Publishing
23847 V66 Trail, Montrose, CO 81403
www.pinyon-publishing.com

Library of Congress Control Number: 2013942966
ISBN: 978-1-936671-17-5

Acknowledgments

Parts of this book have been published far and near in forms both print and electronic, and I have kissed every cover possible for the amazing publishing gift given to me and to so many other fantastical writers swimming in the rough and lumpy magic soup of this tasty world. No way to recall all magazine names, but some were: *Concho River Review, Pinyon Review, Harbinger Asylum, Fringe Magazine, On Barcelona, Gulf Coast, La Noria, Fuck Fiction,* and *Humpty Dumpty.*

I wish to thank Susan Elliott and Gary Entsminger for the gift of such precise editing on this book. They evinced a dedication to the task far beyond the call of duty.

This book is dedicated to Charles Baudelaire and to his
great book, *Paris Spleen*.

It is also dedicated to the lovely members of my family.
We know who we are.

CONTENTS

Introduction   3

Alphabetical Soup   5

Artist of Shadows   7

Begin   8

Beyond Dead Days   9

Buddha Bodacious   11

California Investment Banking   13

Chicken Crossed the Road   14

Clouds   16

Cobalt Blue   18

Crazy   19

Don't Expect Much; I'm Your Postmodern
Milton   21

Dress   22

Drive, He Said   24

Engaged   25

Enraptured Poet Wordsworth, since You claimed the
Child is Father of the Man,   26

Farts and Tears   27

Fly Hope   29

Framing   30

Ghose Dance   32

Ghost out of a Machine   34

Ha!   37

Habit   39

Harrumph   40

Hell   41

History with Snow   43

However Brief   45

Irene Heard There's a Good Black Hole Next Door.
Let's Go   47

Is this Love?   48

Isn't It, Jack   49

Isabel finds that   51

I've Always Considered Shyness a Grave   53

Jerk   55

Johnny   56

King and Queen   58

Knowing   60

Lifeless as a Park Bench Bum   61

Lightness of Being   63

Lucinda   64

Lucky   67

Lucky To Be   69

Man   72

Mirror Lipstick   73

Miss Lonely Heart   74

Moodist   76

Mother was Randy   77

My Former Beloved,   79

My Room   82

Narrative   83

Nature   84

Nature Hike   85

Never Dreamed   87

No Funny Business   88

Normal   93

Not to Talk About   94

Now You Know. Now You Know How it is.   96

On Justice   101

Order of the Sweaty Palms   103

Out By Munson Creek   105

Outgunned   110

Perfectibility   111

Poor Prose Poem   114

Puritan   115

Query   117

Question   118

Reader as Ann Landers   119

Remembering Freud   120

Restless as a Windshield Wiper Blade   121

San Antonio Fish Man   123

Sandy   125

Scholar   128

Shake It   131

Techniques for Revising Above the Real   132

The Trouble with Nature   133

The Unsung   134

Truth   135

Understanding Needed   136

Understanding the Amazon   138

Unexamined Life   139

Unlyric Essay   140

Vantage of Innocence   143

Virgin Manifesto   145

War   148

War Dream   152

Weak Bladder   155

Why I Love Prose Poems   156

Xerox This, Friend   158

Xylophone of Love   159

You may wonder why   162

Youth   164

Zealous   165

Zero Sum   169

Zip-a-Dee-Doo-Dah, My Oh My What a
Wonderful Day   172

Biographical Frame   175

abcdefghijklmnopqrstuvwxyz   177

"The Most difficult thing but an essential one—is to love Life, to love it even while one suffers, because Life is all, Life is God, and to love Life means to love God."

— Leo Tolstoy, *War and Peace*

"Thank the gods that narrative is the illegitimate sire of the joke,"

— Chuck Taylor, *Magical, Fantastical, Alphabetical Soup*

INTRODUCTION

Welcome readers and recreational vehicle enthusiasts, scholars and Scots, housewives or househusbands, the healed, the hungry and the happy, comedians and cornhuskers, romantics and ruffians, pedants and podiatrists, welcome ALL to this zesty alphabetical brew.

Sample this meal of words any way you want. Start with the letter F, or the letter Z, or the letter H. You are not locked in, a slave to the front to back movement of ordinary fictional plot. Merely pick a letter from the alphabet on the alphabetically arranged table of contents. You are like a child before a warm bowl of alphabet soup. Slip your spoon into the steamy broth and stir, and then sample whatever mysteriously floats onto your mental spoon.

It's scrumptious and at times, I hope, entertainingly thoughtful, scandalous, grumpy, humorous, ridiculous, amazingly magical and fantastical. Like the child, try not to be weighted down by too many predetermined notions of what narrative should be. Taste and be free.

"The letter **A**, first letter of the alphabet, is derived from the first letter of the Proto-Sinaitic alphabet: the aleph, which means ox in Semitic languages. So in the beginning, an ox appeared!"

—Ouaknin, *Mysteries of the Alphabet*

Alphabetical Soup

A word first overheard, then whispers and more whispers—
the man has a toupee, Allan is
Bald except around the sides. Now they are laughing,
covering mouths, laughing in a
Cuckoo ridiculous way that starts to expand to fill the
room at the company party as
Delicious snacks are served. The poor man, in his sixties,
begins to plot revenge against
Everyone as his enzymes begin to boil, Allan is a Deacon
in his Baptist Church but he's
Forgetting that for a moment, forgetting the hell and
damnation sermons that are always the
Grand subjects of Preacher Art who is as bald as he is but
no one laughs at him. This will
Haunt Allan in his dreams. So what if Allan wears a rug?
Women wear powder and lipstick.
Is that any less vanity? What of the peroxide or henna or
other stuff, that so many women
Jimmy into their hair to have more fun or to cover up
hideous grey? Why no laughter at them?
Killing seems too kind for these, but then Allan remembers
that he has a young gal
Lover, Alma's nineteen and does not love him but Allan
doesn't that much care, loves her
Monstrously, moonstruckly, sure Alma's too young and in
a few years will fly the coop,
Not meant for him but she's new to the country, broke,
and needs the three room place
Over the garage he's let her stay in the two months she's
worked at the donut shop. He
Pulled his truck over as she walked down Swiss Avenue

and asked if she were Mexican,

Quite clearly she was young and a runaway carrying those plastic bags with all her stuff,

Run away from her family and small home town, without papers, here no cousins or uncles,

Seeking her fortune in Dallas, growing lonely and desperate, no one but this old bald man

To talk to with his blue eyes who acts gentlemanly and kind and speaks good Spanish, so

Unlike the anxious, determined young men who pursued her in the plaza back home,

Very dark, unlike how she is; he's only this old bald man who works for a big company,

Works as a maintenance ox moving from building to building fixing lights and toilettes,

Xenophobic in his hatred of other races, it seems, but deeply smitten, in love with her

Young mocha skin, she's so "exotic" and makes him feel young again, not bald. Allan falls asleep

ZZZ on top of her and Alma dreams of home and hopes, tapping fingers on his bald head.

Artist of Shadows

Artist of the night in his room, the lamp lit, the fan running—white noise to block exterior sounds—the blinds shut tight; artist of the shadows of heart, the strange beatings inside, the mind waking with extraordinary thoughts, worries best kept to oneself, the others in the house sleeping, they've heard it all, over and over, so let him suffer his insomnia rage, a tough old ox alone, artist of the shadows, his books on the walls, his touchstones easily pulled off the shelf, a passage read, his laptop's blue glow, tap, tap, words on the screen out in the night onto the Web for other artists of shadows who seek what they do not know, who dream of a good night's sleep, dazzling energy for the dazzling new day but have forgot that way of being, move through the next day in a molasses way, lost and not remembering, knowing the moments of clarity will return at night when they wake and sleep, wake and sleep, wake and finally for an hour or two receive a buoyant energy, and then the mind turns to fog again and they must try again to sleep. Strange life. Alone life. He whispers phrases, "I'm through with this," "I can't go on any longer." He takes the dog for a walk. The artist of the shadows. He returns and climbs in bed. He writes a rant. It's four a.m. He strokes his aching legs, gets up and takes a pill hoping the aches might cease and he can find oblivion and then amazing dreams.

Begin

Begin the poem with begin and see where begin goes,
the alpha has already cranked itself up into the blue
so this poem will roll out of bed with the day but
where will it go, what will the first words be out of the
mouth, what will be brought to mind that can be taken
as command by the will, or will this poem bop back
on the mattress, close its eyes and try to sleep away?
Do you begin your begin with no where, rub the star
rust out of your eyes and bluster who am I, and am
I happy, and why do problems beset like black stains
on the carpet that won't come out? Should you get
dressed and get in your car and drive, keep going with
no destination in mind, will you find yourself standing
surprised with bouquets of flowers in your hands and
no flames in the dark?

Oh, so, this poem decides finally to get bound up and
face the faces of those it loves and hopes are small
tender sparrows to land on the shoulders of the day
with Saint Francis all smiles, this poem begins shoving
aside duties, acting immature soon, always the baby at
heart, all it wants is a quiet corner in an old bus stop
café, say around 1955, where it can sip coffee out of
a china cup and observe customers in their bountiful
raincoat words and behaviors because it's raining
lonely satellites outside, this poem wishes it could
blast cancer and stop worldwide atomic Armageddon
with the constant B-52's in the big sky, and who knows
maybe in its irresponsible alphabetical byway, it can
and does.

Beyond Dead Days

Dr. Benigni invented, for the end of the semester in colleges throughout the United States, DEAD DAYS. The good doctor has moved beyond to a new, bigger project. He has never been impressed with those trying to invent a machine for time travel. What Benigni actually wants is a machine that can kill time beyond one or two dead days. Kill time as God obliterated the soul of Lilith in the Garden of Eden. Marijuana, Benigni knows, is a means to slow down time; alcohol causes time to speed up, but what if a person could carry a small machine, shaped like a pistol, by which they could kill time? The human lifespan is longer than most animals. We are adults by twenty-one. If the average lifespan in industrialized countries with good national health insurance is somewhere around 78, do we really need fifty-seven years of adult time? It only takes eighteen to twenty-one years to bring up the next generation. If we start late, at thirty, we should be done, if we limit ourselves to bambinos two years apart, by the time we are fifty-three. Why a quarter century more of years consuming the resources when we could carry a small machine to kill time. Two days ago, for instance, my dog became ill. Last night he died while at the veterinarian's. I had to bring him home in a large cardboard box, dig a hole—quite a deep hole because he was a big dog—and then hold a little ceremony over the grave for my wife, my daughter, and myself. We spent a good deal of time crying. No one slept that night. It would have been handy if I could have gotten out Dr. Benigni's machine and killed that time, cut it out from the great blue ribbon of time, like you crop a photograph, or splice out a section of a movie that does not add much to the story. Think of the efficiencies! I don't claim to have an understanding of time on the level of Dr. Benigni. Is it curved? Does it speed up the slower you go, and slow down as you approach the speed of light? Time is clearly much more than what our five senses tell us, or what our culture tells us. Time I tend to think of as toothpaste coming out of the tube, and the hand that squeezes the toothpaste is the great hand of the Big Sky Bopper, but I know my perception is primitive, a writer's perception, not a scientist's. So I am here to propose we start a fund to support Dr. Benigni's research on killing time. He can be reached in care of the publisher. Send any amount you feel is appropriate, small or large. I promise, in this case, you won't be killing time. In this case your time will be well spent.

Buddha Bodacious

A little explored area of history is the Buddhist crusades. Armies of fighting Buddhists, including the famous Bruce Lee the First, used judo, kendo, aikido, and Tae Kwon Do, to attack the holy lands of India and capture the sacred Bo tree under which Buddha meditated, went into rapture, and bopped up to nirvana. After days in nirvana Buddha chose to return, passing through ten thousand blades in order to bring the wisdom to the rest of us.

Of course the Buddhist fighting monks had to rape and pillage along the route of their crusades to maintain themselves body and soul. Sometimes they even had to destroy a Buddhist kingdom or two to get their hands on the needed cash and weapons in a king's treasury. The sacred real estate was captured and held by means of a line of stone forts for twenty-five years, but the religion was ultimately unsuccessful in reestablishing itself in the land of its origin because of the hostility of the native pagan population, the Hindus. Even Buddhist children—children, mind you, full of sweet innocence and fervor—were unsuccessful in moving the pagans toward the true blue light of his truth during the Buddhist children's crusades. The Buddhist crusades did however establish lasting ruling elites in Tibet, Bhutan, and Mongolia.

Use of the blade of conversion comes down to the present day, in a loose network of Buddhist terrorists known as Buddha Bodacious, headed by a shadowy figure hiding in the deep jungle forests of present day Laos. The Buddha Bodacious may or may not be responsible for the unreported bombing of the heretical communist capital of Beijing, in an effort, during the recent Olympics, to restore the Dalai Lama and free Tibet.

California Investment Banking

We all had black faces—buy me municipal bonds, no taxes on those, clients called and called—but we were making way too much money to let our faces show. Ka-ching, ka-ching, the sound faster and faster like a spinning windmill in a hurricane. We always had black faces. We were born with black faces. We liked our black faces. Our wives claimed we were comely. I talk on the phone. "It's them Jews," one client says, "them Jews, them liberal New York Jews who control government and want to raise taxes." I talk on the phone. It's a millionaire farmer from the valley. Cal owns large shares in power companies from San Diego to Seattle. "Too dang many Catholics," Cal says. "Just because they pick fruit in the summers they think they should be citizens. They reproduce like rabbits. The Pope's out to capture the whole world. Buy me t-bills, five hundred thousand in t-bills. The market's going crazy and I need a place that's safe."

Our accents and our grammar ring college correct. We have our black faces, but we're making too much cash to let them show. The stories I could tell you, the stories I'm leaving out, the things people said without knowing who we were, it turned our stomachs and made our blood boil, but ah the money was so good back then. My partner, my brother, he called a plastic surgeon. "I can cut off your black faces," he said, "but all you'd be left with are terrible scars."

Chicken Crossed the Road

It was dusk. You love the dusk land, when neither the eye's cones nor rods are operating at full capacity, when the world seems to have climbed to the top of a hill facing the sunset and wonders if it has the energy to roll down. Dusk is poised. It is hovering, and the chicken has started to cross the road.

You are driving in your cool Chrysler convertible down a paved Highway 696 and have passed through the tiny community of Clovis. You like chickens. You used to keep them and fell in love with their pedantic ways, but the radio is on to an old fifty's song called "Get a Job," and you have one hand on the wheel and are singing the chorus nonsense line, "da, da, da da; da da da da, da," when you catch a white feathered flash of a chicken and slam on your breaks.

That gives the chicken enough time to cross part of the road and get out of your lane, but then the chicken does something, in its pedantic way, that is so touchingly human: it senses that there is trouble, and when there is trouble, well, it makes sense that you should stop going the way you are going and reverse yourself.

The chicken does a fast, awkward 180-degree turn and takes fast wide steps, so that it is in perfect position for your front passenger side wheel to run over. Blink. Just like that. Crushed.

"The chicken's death was quick," an angel whispers.

You know it was only a chicken. You've eaten thousands of chickens. They're stupid animals. A farmer once told you that they will drown themselves, their mouths wide open and pointed up into the rain of cloudy sky.

"But it was a free-range chicken," the other angel speaks. "You are always quoting Albert Schweitzer on reverence for life. Albert wouldn't even swat a mosquito in the act of biting him. A sect of Hindus in India wears special veils to keep from inhaling insects. Some Jain saints have followers who sweep the ground with fallen peacock feathers so they will not step and crush an insect."

You pull off the road where the shoulder grows wider. You look for signs of the chicken on your tire, your bumper, your wheel well. Nothing. You open your hood and scrape off all the moth and butterfly bits of wings you can identify amongst all the bug protoplasm. You gather the broken bits and set them on a small pyre of twigs you've made that you light with a lighter.

You imagine yourself an Indian and sing what you believe to be calm death and mourning songs in the now dark, what with the clear and brilliant stars overhead, and a light breeze blowing. You dream respect for the living and the dead.

Clouds

Clara used to photograph clouds, all kinds of clouds. She'd shoot them at an angle to catch in the corner of the photo something of the earth, to give context, to contrast our pitiful human constructions with her favored floating palaces. She has this great shot of the Texas State Capital—a splendid classical construction, larger than the US Capital—but nothing compared to her Notre Dames of the sky. Clouds look so stunning, climbing like mountains in a pure billowy white up the overwhelming infinite of the sky's intense blue. They drift and shift with such calm and magnificent dignity, like a grand and mysterious white whale cruising through the great Pacific seas.

Ah, but my Clara flew to Chicago for her first major gallery show. It was her first airplane flight—can you believe? What a blow to her aesthetics, her dreams and her hopes. The plane dropped from 40,000 feet down into the flat grey wall of winter clouds near Lake Michigan. She learned, when the plane went inside the clouds, that they were merely fog and more fog, on and on, seemingly endless, unchanging and boring.

My love might have been better off not flying, not knowing the bitter disappointment of clouds that seem so alive but have no blood or heart. Thank God I had purchased copies of her wonderful work, at decent prices before she became famous, and before she trashed her digital files. Clara grew depressed. She didn't know if she could ever trust her own creations again, if all she had been doing was imposing her own inner dreams and hopes on externals that were never made to take on her private obsessions.

I, I have her photographs on my walls. Clara dislikes coming to my place and asks me to take her photographs down. "I seek truth, not illusion," she tells me. I ask her what I should put on my walls. Does she have something new? I can dream still of white towering castles, shape-shifting against the great and infinite blue. My love, all she says in her moody ways these days, is that she hopes she has not discovered a parable. Here in our life on earth we see daily miracles, the complex and colored diversity of infinite forms, but what if grey is the final color for all the corridors of life?

Cobalt Blue

The cedars in my neighbor's yard enjoy each other's company on cool October mornings. A lot of silence sings in these cedars, a lot of stillness, and some slow motions and whispering. Trees are some of my favorite companions and I often stop when walking my border collie to converse with trees. I am more comfortable in a crowd of trees than in a crowd of people. People crowded on elevators, standing straight and silent, on long upward rides in big city buildings, take on the dignity of forests. I've yet to have a single soul try to convert me to their brand of religion, or their brand of politics, while climbing into the calm sky inside an elevator. No one has asked me to serve on a committee. No one has read me a prose poem colored cobalt blue.

Crazy

The woman I loved lived in the woods on the edge of Austin in an underground cave, I guess you would call it. She dug a hole at the top of a hill and put boards across and then she put plywood and covered the wood with dirt. Since she was at the top of this small hill hidden in the scrub of the woods no one ever noticed her though there was a trail thirty feet away where the joggers passed and the people walked with dogs on leashes down to the shore of Cripple Creek. Rain didn't creep into her home much either because of the hill.

The woman had in her youth been a crooner and then a philosophy major who could read Kant in the original German but now she lived in the woods and got cash by going to churches and asking for money though sometimes they gave her jobs cutting lawns. I had never loved an older woman before and she had acquired a kind of wisdom that time seems to bestow almost automatically. I really had the hots for her. She kept her poems in a pile on a rock and I'd bring mine and we'd recite poems sitting on cool rocks along the shore of Cripple Creek. All the time I'd be thinking of her naked.

She had some crazy spots in her brain—we all have those spots—but things went fine as long as I kept away from her crazy spots and she stayed away from mine, and we were both sane enough to do that. My crazy spots all had to do with numbers. Basically I am at odds with the way numbers are used by the

19

government and corporations to control us and the world. I find numbers more controlling than atom bombs. Numbers should be abolished or at least kept in prison.

The woman I loved kept an old lover in her head who she claimed she saw each day, but sometimes she would bump into two or three guys who were imposters of her man Clem. It was almost impossible to tell the real Clem from the imposters except over time because the imposters did not love her while the real Clem did. I didn't dare say this long narrative lived only in her head. The woman I loved was faithful to Clem, so she and I remained merely companions.

Things might have gone along good forever that way — I see now — but I made the mistake of consulting those damn numbers. I could see my odds were slim. She wouldn't even let me claim a kiss, so I left behind those cool lovely woods and the woman who was their spirit along Cripple Creek and I never once went back. Now it's been maybe seven years. One day I'll get some librarian not afraid of numbers to check on the Internet to see if she's still kicking.

Don't Expect Much; I'm Your Postmodern Milton

The author Dougal is tired. He ate sashimi for supper in a fancy Japanese restaurant in Denton and now it moves through his bowels like a large sailor's knot. Dougal begins to keep track of time in his dreams by the pain's movement, and when he wakes and gives up trying to sleep at four a.m., he grabs his notebook from the night stand (no light, so as not to wake his love), and he thinks, you know, I've got a grand figure going here—that time with love at your side is like pain moving through the dark bowels of the universe. Dougal peeks under the curtain and whispers to the stars, *What do you think of that—more than you expected, huh?* AND ISN'T LAUGHTER THE OPPOSITE OF PAIN? the author jots in his notebook. And when we laugh with our love, don't we interrupt, in the radiant jiggle and guffaw of flesh, the doleful flow of time?

Dress

Everyone, at least once in his or her life, should wear a dress. Now Drew's known a few men who wear dresses regularly, and others who get dressed up on special occasions. Sinclair Lewis got drunk at a Minnesota party; he went upstairs to the hostess's closet and picked out an evening gown to impress the flappers. A certain filmmaker, whose name Drew thinks was Ed Wood, not only revived the dead career of horror actor Béla Lugosi but would also drop into a dress whenever stressed. For a moment he'd turn into a luxurious Hollywood doll and his tensions would evaporate. Here is a solution much healthier than heroin or Scotch.

Drew goes for the classical styles made of 100% cotton. He digs bright flower patterns. When you wear a dress it's like you've left the front door open inviting whatever animal passing by to stop in. Your legs develop a relationship to the intimate drafts flowing down by the floor. They are whispering to you all their secrets, what they've picked up wandering down the hallways, from room to room, across rivers and ponds, deserts and mountains. The dress is the opposite of armor. It displays both your vulnerability and your trust. A dress is also a dance of the seven veils, or can be—more flowing, less bold and stiff than a slit skirt, less suggestive of bondage. If Drew were a woman he'd never wear dresses or skirts. He would worship pants as a god. Throughout most of recorded history a huge sign in the sky made of iron dangled above over women, YOU MUST WEAR A DRESS.

The world doesn't deserve women wearing dresses. The world contains way too much dope, rape, destruction, and war. But women don't think about it. They persevere, they continue to love, leaving themselves open for what begins life and what bears life, when they step out into the light wearing, like petals of a sunflower opening, a dangerous dress.

Drive, He Said

For Robert Creeley

Drake's got a San Antonio Spurs cap down to his
eyebrows. He's getting up there in years, Drake is,
with shaking jowls and a thinning spot at the back of
his head. He sits low in the seat so you can barely see
his eyebrows over the dash.

I'm talking about my neighbor, the alcoholic across the
street, who I've watched backing out of his driveway,
often unsteadily, for years. I've even put my life at
risk riding along on a few of his drives from our dry
country to Lake Tawakoni for cases of beer.

For a while Drake tried to make a living repairing old
refrigerators out of his garage, but lately he's been
coasting, living off his nurse wife. Sometimes, after
a fight, Drake goes outside and sits in his pickup for
hours, as if the truck were his only place of refuge,
his only home, as if he's debating whether to stay or
to go. His teenage daughter Dolores will look out her
bedroom window and sometimes start to cry.

When Drake and I make the drive for beer, I never
mention the various songs of birds that sometimes
make their way inside the cab, or the tragedies of the
thunderclouds drifting high above the low hills. He
knows what he knows. Hold to the road in the dirt of
time. Get in and drive.

Engaged

Ennis could be thinking of how he is loved, but no, Ennis is thinking of Henry the Eighth's ceremonial armor ever on display in the Tower of London.

Ennis could be thinking of how he is loved, yes, but instead he studies the elaborate patterns of design on Henry the Eighth's armor, Ennis sees the expanse of steel at the waste to allow for his paunch, Ennis has a paunch and he wonders if it bothered Henry to put on his armor — or did he ever put on his armor? What age was he when he would have entered this machine of war?

Ennis can see the little carved and decorated cup with the hinge at the V where the legs begin that allowed the great king to pull out his royal member to take a piss, the royal member that failed to produce a legitimate male heir for him, the poor, murderous king, who never ever knew the honest amour of a woman, who was so armored in sovereignty, so invulnerable, that he may have moved early in life beyond hope, beyond even caring, to be engaged purely by pleasure and the use of power.

Enraptured Poet Wordsworth, since You claimed the Child is Father of the Man,

Ethan wanted you to know he's good at dodging balls, and that's because of his ma. It's hard to hit him with a snowball or volleyball. Ethan's agile and can dodge easily with his limber, thin frame this way and that. And Ethan's fearless—has never been smacked by a pitcher from the mound by a fast ball, as he stood crowding the plate, hoping to whack a home run on a pitch thrown high and wide back in Little League. No pitcher could dust him off and it's all due to his mother, who loved to throw hairbrushes at his head starting back when he was in the first grade. Suppose Ethan had not cleaned his room in a month in spite of warnings; she'd storm in screaming, clutching a hairbrush from the bathroom, and launch it at his head. She was a good shot, but Ethan would leap aside and the brush would smack against the wall. Ah, the skills acquired from parents. The family had a whole batch of plastic hairbrushes with their handles broken off. Ethan could still comb his hair with them, even though they'd been thrown at his head. An adult now, he thinks of his ma, and never makes his bed.

Farts and Tears

Fabian has no objection to women crying. It doesn't make him nervous at all. Fabian rather enjoys the fine music of tears because Fabian likes to cry himself and keeps a box of tissues in his office for protection.

Let's you and Fabian bawl out one fantastic gulley washer! You know how it hurts Fabian just as much to fire you as it hurts you. Crying is as natural as farting. When men refuse to cry, they get heart problems. When women refuse to fart, they get stomach troubles. A tissue works fine for both. A little air freshener may be needed, although Fabian's father simply burned a match to mask the smell.

Do women cry more as they get older? Men sure do fart more. Men are from Mars. They become old farts and boom away—the term old fart is not an insult, merely descriptive. The compensation is the farts lose their malevolent odor and become neutral. We need more farts in the movies and on television, at least as many farts as tears. Unlike crying, farting always makes you feel better. The president, of course, should lead the way as General Schwarzkopf did with prostate examinations and Bob Dole did with erectile dysfunctions. One good blast at the first and finale of his State of the Union Address would demonstrate fine macho prowess and taboos would tumble like so many shopping carts in a hurricane. Farting would become as acceptable as crying, only another natural function emanating from the temple of our bodies. The first woman president, or the first African-American

27

president, could go down in history for far more than gender or race.

Fly Hope

There's a small fly that, like a World War I biplane, dives at those pesky, stinging imported fire ants we so adore as they forage our yards and gardens for food to kill and eat. The ant knows the fly means him no good and will try to hide under a blade of grass or a leaf, or the ant will scurry back to his home in the mound. The Brazilian creature is about half the size of our ordinary housefly. It has a spiked and slightly curved ovipositor that can quickly slip an egg inside a fire ant at a small break between the armor plates on the ant's thorax. The egg hatches into a larva, and the larva eats the inside of the ant until it reaches a size where it can barely crawl through into the ant's head. There the larva eats on the ant's brain, using the ant's skull as protection from such outside enemies as birds. When it reaches the right size, the larva bites through a ligament that causes the ant's head to fall off. The larva crawls out and shortly thereafter turns into a fly.

In this science I've found an allegory for the ordinary human's current condition. The fire ant is some part of the toxic, earth devouring, society you must live in and feed from. You are the larva in the belly of what is actually a well armored, poisonous, but surprisingly vulnerable, beast. By such stealth you can survive and are a potent adversary indeed.

Framing

This narrative—in spite of its shape—is completely unframed. Instead of imagining the white that surrounds as a frame, or a box that holds these words in this little rectangular space like a lovely nude on the front wall above a bar, see the expanse of white as wide open. We words, like Aristotle said, are social creatures and prefer to flock together like female elephants to form meaning. Still, watch this: we can at any time flip out of our sociability and sense; we can step outside the box, venture into wild fields of snow or fine sandy deserts, we know there are oases filled with shade and water, so here we go, yes, in any moment now some sister or brother words are going to stick toes out and test the weather in the beyond, an adventure like Columbus sailing for the new world. Money to be found, people to enslave, so here we go! Are you ready? One, two, and three and we're out!

The blue scarf of a river formed around the arm of the void. The void voided itself to avoid paying frangible angelic taxes. The sociable trees flapped their leaves and barked approval.

Pretty impressive, huh? Hey, hold on, I think something's wrong. Does anyone actually find themselves out in another reality? I did, but only for a moment. A glitch might be in the program. Now you may think I'm trying to frame the issue, to convince you that the narrative can set you free, or you may think I am trying to make narrative a central issue of public debate, but I don't give a flying Frisbee purchased at a dollar store what you think about narrative, though

Muriel Rukeyser said something to the effect that the world is not made of atoms; it is made of stories. Stories are older than you and I and will be around long after we've flown the coop. I mean, if voting could change the system, it wouldn't be legal, right? Narratives have been around, like I said, for a long time and know the score and work hard not to go flabby. Did you catch this year's Paris runway with its hot fashions? Well, let me tell you, narrative is twenty years ahead of that. But I'm not trying to frame the issue. You do not have to start thinking you're not cool if you do not find a narrative in your back pocket, understand? No sweat off my back. Why should I give a frickin' foolscap — but unfortunately I do.

Ghose Dance

Would you believe? Seven out of ten times a body opened the door and came in — Ghose could tell which section of the store they'd go to and what kind of books they'd buy. Those who bought medieval history could easily be recognized by their glum and hooded eyes.

Would you believe? Six out of ten, Ghose could tell which windows would bulge out like a fish eye and explode scattering glass everywhere when a great building was gouged by fire. Those that exploded tended to be those that had grown tired of their own clarity.

Would you believe? Five out of ten, Ghose could tell which cars, when traveling down a lonesome road, would gravitate to being large birds or airplanes to lift off in flight. Looking at their grills it is possible to make out the grimaced pain, that they no longer wished to be concerned with the grinding steel of the human prospect.

Would you believe? Four out of ten times, Ghose can get on an airplane with a catcher's mitt and bucket in his carry-on, go to the right city, taxi to the right field, and within ten minutes of standing there alone listening to the music of birds Ghose does not see, he can grab a meteor out of the sky flaming down. The mitt of course catches fire and Ghose has to throw the mitt down into the water filled bucket he's got at his feet.

Ghose knows you want to believe, though it's part of your nature to both believe and not believe. You might be one of those who would sacrifice a great fortune to see a loaf turned into a fish.

Ghost out of a Machine

Ghislaine never could get it, the bright aura that glowed off of personal computers in the old days, but everyone else, or almost everyone else, swore by it, except a few skeptics like herself. On the front of the telephone book in 1991 they did a naked baby, private parts discretely hidden by a leg, reaching out in the halo glow of a large computer screen, about to touch its glass.

Imagine her surprise, then, when in 1997 the college students moved out of the house next to hers and a computer was left at the curb, to be hauled off by the garbage collectors. Ghislaine figured the computer might get rained on before pickup day, so she lugged the various components inside to a desk kept in the living room. In 1997 Ghislaine still did not own a computer, but she'd learned the basics on a machine given to her at her office.

Her husband and daughter would be overjoyed to have at last a computer. Would Ghislaine tell them she'd found it in the trash? Her family was not at home at the time, so Ghislaine hooked up the component parts, plugged the machine in, and booted up. The main processing unit with the hard drive still looked like little more than a pile of steel to her, reminiscent of the metal wastebaskets of the 1970's. As a matter of fact, her office still had the same metal wastebasket from when Ghislaine started working in insurance in 1974. When Ghislaine was a teenager in the early 1960's, they told pregnant women not to sit close to television

34

screens. Now people, including her, were ruining eyes, their noses glued up to the cathode ray tube grafted on computers.

Ghislaine clicked on the My Computer icon and checked the applications folder—the usual programs, no game files—and then she checked the documents folder. There was one document on the computer. Curious about the life of her former neighbors, Ghislaine opened the document and read it. What she found was an unsigned letter written by a pregnant college woman to her unborn child, explaining why she'd had her child aborted. It had been an unplanned pregnancy from a one-night stand. Ghislaine cried easily, and she almost cried when she finished the woman's two-page letter, but then Ghislaine felt guilty for violating the unknown woman's privacy and moved the two-page document to the trash. But then, she took the letter out of the trash and hid it in the applications file.

Her family ended up using the computer going on five years. She'd write on it, and her husband would send emails. Their daughter added a few games she played, but they were determined to make sure their daughter did not become a computer addict and would instead spend her time with them, read books, or play with her friends. Ghislaine still has the computer stored in the attic of the garage.

Ghislaine has a digital camera and stores pictures on

her laptop. Her daughter is in high school and they have a more up to date machine for her to use on school projects. Ghislaine must admit however that she still had not seen the ghost of God in either the computer or the Internet. Let her, instead, take you down the street to a vacant lot. There she'll show you Queen Anne's Lace, show you primroses and buttercups, if it is the right season.

And oh, Ghislaine needs to mention the child. Ghislaine did not know the names of the students who then lived next door. New batches continue to come every year — but the child, the document left unsigned, in that document you need to know that the child was given a name — Geraldine.

You may think it's strange, but one late afternoon — Ghislaine surprised herself — one day after Ghislaine'd mowed the backyard, she got her husband's pocketknife out of his drawer and carved the child's name into the white bark of a water oak tree. Ghislaine put a heart around her name, and below "Geraldine," Ghislaine carved the words "and Mom."

Ha!

The world would be a hell of a better place if they'd televise more prose poems. Don't put them on public television; the audience remains too small. Suitable sponsors, Hannah's convinced, can be found among the traditional broadcast channels and the cable stations. One can segue seamlessly, say, between the prose poems and dancing hamburgers in a McDonald's jingle.

Product placement also can be carried off in prose poems both huge and short. The firecracker moon sparkles with Eveready batteries. The butterflies of Ambien sleep. Old products can be placed and brought back to life. I'm thinking of the Burma Shave jingles on little red wooden signs you'd pass on the highways back in the 1950's. *Go Ahead and Be Brave / To that ugly beard you're not a slave / Wave and whip out the Burma Shave!*

Televise your most carefully scripted prose poems during prime time. Make prose poems so they are pop-ups on computers. Certainly you've noticed the lack of sex and violence in most prose poems. They'd be perfect for Saturday morning kids shows. Little animal puppets can speak their lines.

Is Hannah going on too long? You're not convinced? Let her share some history.

Can anyone in the room name the greatest prose poem ever televised?

IT GOES BACK, IT GOES BACK MAYBE FORTY YEARS—the prose poem that could be translated into any language, the prose poem that soldiers recited wearing ear plugs that was so funny the enemy would fall dead in their trenches convulsed with laughter. According to Monty Python, it was a British top-secret weapon, perfect for conventional wars but not so good for guerrilla wars like today's Iraq, where you don't want the collateral damage like what you get with suicide bombers or drones.

Who's laughing when you can't tell the enemy from the people you've come to save? Prose poems are too often humorous, and hardly ever should be used by a modern military.

Habit

When Handel found himself yearning like a Romeo, acting like some moon-besotted youth, he couldn't help but imagine himself on a leafy Austin backstreet, close to the capital building, east of I-35, stretched out on the carpet with a greasy wall to support his back, lighting a crack pipe.

Drugs are so romantic. Directors say it's impossible to make an anti-war movie. War looks so bloody exciting up on the silver screen.

Judging from musicians Handel has known who became heroine addicts after reading William Burroughs's *Naked Lunch*, he'd argue it's impossible to write a novel that does not romanticize addictive drugs.

Imagine the adventurous ups and downs of losing your teeth and losing your house to maintain your hellish methamphetamine habit. It's so biblical; the last become first.

Handel walks certain wisdom. A PhD candidate in philosophy at the University of Texas, he traded his precious, heavily marked, copy of Hume for some high quality crystal meth.

Harrumph

Have you had the chance to visit nursing homes? They're going extinct, thanks to the Republicans' love for free markets, but you should while there's still a chance.

Around every corner you will hear the voice of God. An old man will be moaning from his wheelchair in the hallway close to the nursing station. An old woman you can't see in her room will fire a string of obscenities as blue and horrific as one of Melville's sailors. She will be answered by a parrot kept in a cage and taken out on occasion to entertain the bed-bound patients.

The woman who shared the room with Harriet's mother — Helen it said at the foot of her bed — slept for four straight years. Now and then Helen would go HARRUMPH and smack her gums. Her husband came only once, yet told Harriet how he was devoting his retired years to taking care of his dear loving wife Helen who had given him six wonderful children.

"Honey," Hilda used to say every time Harriet headed for her mother's room, "Honey, would you open that door for me?" Hilda moved slowly toward the light from the window in the door using her walker, but she had a metal band around her wrist that made the door lock as soon as she reached it.

Harriet has no trouble keeping faith here. Rumi writes that you can hear God in the chained dog howling for its master.

Hell

Writers write about hell all the time. Hell this, hell that. They grind their teeth and chew their knuckles, but complacent Herman knows the concept of hell haunts his head only once a decade, at the maximum, when he thinks about his mother's suicide attempts or his grandfather's atheism. The earth's a finite ball in space, and we've done enough deep drilling to conclude it's too full of molten rock to support a home for demons.

"My self am hell," Milton had his Satan say. Herman knows hell can be a psychological condition you carry around in your head, and he's carried it, unaware that the locks are spring-loaded and at any moment he probably could have hopped free. At times others came along and set him free, a bit like Donald Trump on television shouting, "You're fired!"

Now heaven, in contrast to hell, keeps expanding on us, and remains unknown, mysterious, beyond comprehension and imagination. The more we know about space, the more sublime it gets and seems to be God, and since earth is part of space it follows that earth is part of God.

That leaves us however with a thorny problem. What do we do with the bad? Can we let them get away with it, with punishment left only to what the state comes up with? In the protestant hell of Herman's neighbors, it's all predestined, determined before you are born, whether you go up or down. This eliminates the legal profession in heaven and helps keep taxes low. His

Catholic neighbors however hold up the chance of working your way up and out, of a burning away of all but the most hellish of sins, but, well, as Herman has already demonstrated, there's no real estate for hell, no habitat.

Christians, Herman believes, should internationalize and believe in reincarnation. Depending on how you behave, you work your way up in successive rebirths, or work your way down. Your timeline in the cycles of death and birth could resemble the chart of the Dow Jones Average. Now that's bringing religion up to date, making it modern.

History with Snow

I haven't been around snow in twenty-eight years, since the time we were goofing off in the hot tub on an Austin December night at New Manor Apartments. We watched the snow quickly build up along the roof around the Christmas lights, and we went right from the hot tub to the swimming pool, whizzing snowballs at each other naked, yes, Trish and I and Harriet and Hillary, heated up by the hot tub so we didn't feel cold—yet if you ask me, do I honestly miss snow now, I would have to answer nay, because I have that great December night, in George Orwell's 1984 nightmare year, and Trish being obsessed, certain with Reagan in office that it was the totalitarian end, but I was too well fed and too in love with my lovely Trish to ever care, but if you ask once more, do I miss snow (many exiled in the South do miss snow), I will have to continue to say nay, I don't miss the heaviness of snow, the dangerous cold, the slippery risks of driving, the back breaking shoveling, and the sooty icy boulder piles left on corners by the midnight noisy plows. No, I don't miss, but I do recall fondly the tingle of snow on your rosy cheeks as you take a slow stroll, and it's lightly coming down in big huffy flakes, the way it gathers like butterflies in your hair and on your shoulders, and the great silence when you wake up on Saturday with no place to go and snow has transformed the whole wide earth. You look out the window at the silhouettes in your driveway—that's a basketball covered in snow, that's Hill's tricycle, and that must be a cardboard box with something inside. You get on your snow gear and dash outside to build snowmen and snow forts and

43

you break into groups and begin the great snowball fights. Oh yes, I recall that, and the taste when you pick up snow fresh in your mittens, put it to the tongue, sweet and cold, and later the full moon shinning high through the black bare branches of trees gilding the snow with a heavenly glow, and you take slow steps in your galoshes and hear, like the breaking of bread, in the cold holy silence under your feet, the crunch, that slow lovely grinding crunch, (Oh sweet Jesus I miss that) of snow, of heavenly given pure new snow, I might miss snow without that fantastical, mystical hot tub Austin December night, all of us naked, with my southern darling Trish, gone now — she left me — in and out of mental confusions, the great love of my life ...

However Brief

Howard's up in the mountains, in San Miguel de Allende, at an arts community two hours east by curving roads from Mexico City. He's come to dream himself a poet amongst artists after four years in Japan where he's been making four thousand a month in salary and two thousand a month on the stock market. Howard's an impractical human, a guy who before Japan hid in the woods in a tent and didn't own a working car.

Howard would never call himself poor. How can he be poor when he's studied Plato's *Republic* and has read all of Chaucer, Faulkner, Shakespeare, and Tolstoy? How he can he be poor when he knows by heart all of Beethoven's nine symphonies, most of Mozart, and Stravinsky's *Rite of Spring*, plus Degas and Van Gogh. No, he can't be poor, but many times he's been low on money, but never so low as not to have something in the cupboard to eat or some homey place to stay.

But now Howard finds himself on a December night in San Miguel, sitting in an outdoor bistro across from the Plaza lit up with Christmas lights, drinking an overpriced Corona beer. His friend Hopper is sitting next to him. Hopper's back from an afternoon of curio shopping and has a bag full of trinkets he won't be able to find in his garage back home in six months, and he's furious at Howard because an Indian boy, about eight years old, carrying his baby sister on his back, came into the café and tried to sell both of them handmade items. Howard has given the boy three hundred dollars

American in Mexican pesos. The boy's hands had started shaking slightly and his body moved, Howard noticed, in a tense and angular way, out of a sudden wonder in the midst of absolute need.

His friend Hopper quotes the Bible, in his high sarcastic way, "The poor will always be with us," stretching out the distance between the Prince of Peace and the people he is speaking of, making it seem a condemnation of charity.

Howard looks across to a side street onto the plaza and sees the boy with his mother. He can tell by their animated movements that they have forgotten him—the foreigner, the old man—but they are happy and are dreaming. A small space of hope, however brief, has opened as if a Saint had come down from heaven and blessed them. As to his friend Hopper, well, he's an emotionally repressed son of the Scottish immigrants. He can't read the map of his own emotions. His sudden shot of anger, Howard knows is momentary jealousy—it hurts when someone does a little good and you are merely your normal flesh of self—but the anger however will be brief, gone in the morning.

Irene Heard There's a Good Black Hole Next Door. Let's Go

Today Irene likes clouds. Tomorrow she could be in the blue trying to bite those floating dirigibles.

Insipid empty things, actually, with their poodle tricks interested in grabbing attention.

Today the big bang theory fits neatly inside the roof of Irene's mouth like a plastic retainer designed by an experienced orthodontist. But tomorrow ... tomorrow ... there's a football game her son plays in and she'll be intense thunderbolts of worry.

You love me she loves you we don't know where if ever our coordinates will meet in this expanding universe taking all the stars away and leaving us only with our singular moon.

Is this Love?

So I'm in front of the Red Box machine waiting to rent a movie, waiting on a young woman as she carefully reads by cell phone the plots of various films to her boyfriend on the other end.

The weather's good in front of the grocery store. I'm in no hurry. I like to watch the people going in and out of the Kroger's Grocery. This woman is on her way home from work. She looks irritated and tired. She has a bottle of wine in a sack standing by her feet.

The boyfriend doesn't like the films the woman's taking time to tell him about. His angry words start to bleed loudly around her ear.

"I love you," she finally says, with the wind of worry in her voice, before she gives an almost invisible shrug and flicks off her phone.

She gives me a slight smile as she walks away, back to her car with her sacks of groceries, without a movie to share.

Isn't It, Jack

I can't tell you all the things I'd be out there protesting, if I had the time, if didn't have work night and day to earn the almighty buck, if I didn't have to fix the car when it breaks down, do laundry and get the boys off to school. And then my wife has to take the bus to the nursing home where she works cause I need my old junk car to drive forty miles to my job in Dallas. Don't think I'm stupid, or don't care, because we haven't made the rent at times. They've put our stuff right on the curb for people to take.

Don't think I don't know what's right because I've spent time in jail for unpaid parking tickets and stuff. Right off I want to say my woman shouldn't have to transfer twice on the Fort Worth buses and leave for work ninety minutes ahead of time if this country had decent transportation. I don't like what's happening with our weather. I know about the tons of shit that's coming out of the butts of these billions of cars and airplanes and trucks. I want an earth that my kids can live on, one where they won't get burned up in searing heat, or die of cancer young from the chemicals we're shooting in the animals we eat and spraying on the crops.

They came along and invented all these machines — not just cars and trucks and planes and atom bombs — but the computers and gizmos in factories that put people out of work, and they said these devices made for more leisure time. They said we'd have more hours to be with our families, but I saw on TV that people are

49

sleeping six hours a night instead of eight, and that'll give them sickness later on in life. What good are all these machines if they muck up the earth and sky and make us have to slave like machines?

Now I'm not against work. I like work. I want to pay my own way. But I love my family too, and I don't like being worried all the time about the rent or if we've got enough to eat. My grandparents lived on a farm and built their own house with their neighbors' help. They grew a lot of their own food. If I had a house I could plant a garden, but I can't afford the rent on such a place. Why can't I get a steady job, so my wife can cut back and spend more time with the boys, and cook them decent food, instead of the fast food crap we end up picking up at a drive through that costs so much. If I had a place to grow some things, I could share with my neighbors and get to know them.

I can't tell you all the shit I'd protest if I had the time and didn't have to stress out struggling for the all mighty dollar, but that's the way it works, and that's the way they want us—broke and suffering, slaves of labor all the time—isn't it, Jack? Isn't it? That's why we now pay for cell phones, at both ends of the line, so we can be doing work for free, off the clock, while driving in our cars, or feeding the kids at home. Isn't it, Jack?

Isabel finds that

weather, more often than not, is either insufferable or boring. We try to avoid its insistent presence as much as possible, and spend a good deal of our energy and money inside doing just that. Weather is like your dentist. You don't like him, yet you know you need him. As Isabel writes this, Isabel thinks of how fortunate that, over the last intolerable summer months, she's been avoiding the weather as much as she can. Wouldn't you, if you had to live in Texas during the era of global warming? Down here in the subtropics, the temperature can run over a hundred for eighty straight days. Is Isabel boring you? She's sorry. It's the weather. But think of the ninety percent humidity inhabiting where Isabel lives. Think of the blazing ultraviolet rays that cause cancer and cataracts. After two months of drought Isabel's got a huge brown splotch of a yard. A post oak, in full leaf, fell over two doors down and it sounded like a meteor striking a roof. Finally it's raining. Isabel hears chops of hail in the midst of the rain drops smacking the shingles, leaving their indentations, but inside it's 72 degrees, as it always is, as it always should be outside, if we had a benevolent deity who so loved the world. Isabel insists he be Gandhi, or even Jesus, but out there dwell volcanoes, tornados, avalanches, earthquakes, droughts, heat waves, cold waves, tsunami's—has Isabel forgot one of these intentions of God? All this when the weather's not being insufferably boring. The serial killer Ted Bundy, in contrast, was a loving, charming man. Oh, yeah, Isabel admits at times she gets a lift from the window looking out into a bed of

roses, but as much as possible, she stays in her boxes—
in her home, her car, her favorite bar, in the stores
she shops in—where humans have established some
semblance of decency, order, and control.

The weather, don't you wish sometimes it were a lost
Happy Meal toy forgotten in the back yard, chewed up
by a dog?

I've Always Considered Shyness a Grave

Ivan likes his study's tiny window although there's too much to see. The window's on the second floor, with mini-blinds down to where a small air conditioning unit sits and then on the shelf before the window sits an intense cow's skull he found the night of the Harmonic Convergence out at Enchanted Rock, before his poet camping buddy Ike knew he was going to die of stomach cancer, when he was saying every ten minutes, "Are we having fun yet?" A car passed by, an older car, Ivan connects with older cars better than with new cars, they seem to have had a life and developed an interesting history; now a man went by on a bicycle, an older man, in his sixties, but mostly what's most prominently framed is the top of a post oak, as a shadow on the neighbor's concrete driveway across the street. Now a car pulls into the driveway, but doesn't stay, only uses the driveway to turn around and go back the way it came. So much life in so little a frame! The grass Ivan sees is singing thanks to the recent rain. A tree in Ivan's yard shimmers with small yellow leaves, his mailbox—the rural style on a pole with a small flag to raise—and one of the same kind on the other side of the street—have been good soldiers standing at attention for twenty years. You'd think they'd be irritated and lonely. They do not cry. Perhaps they tell each other informing and wise stories. The phone rang downstairs but Ivan's not going to answer it. He hears somebody talking into the answering machine, a woman's voice, no doubt for his wife. Ivan feels bad because a man knocked on the door a few minutes ago wanting to cut his grass and tend his yard. Ivan knows his yard looks eccentric but he enjoys the exercise of keeping it the way it is. These guys probably think they're going to make a tidy sum cutting down the dead tree in his yard and wouldn't understand if Ivan said he's got a chain saw in the garage and some rope and has never taken down a dead tree but wants to read up on it and do it once before he dies. The men who knock are always poor men, and if Ivan were to tell them all the money he has to last the month's final six days are in a closet coin jar, they wouldn't believe him. It's four o'clock on a Friday afternoon, another car went down his street, the temperature is about sixty-eight degrees on this October twenty-fourth day, two thousand eight, the shadow of the tree top on the driveway has shifted like the moon, moved into the street, now here comes another car, a green mini-van. Such a small window, such a tiny view on the world and it's too much, it pains Ivan, all that insists on hitting his senses, demonstrating it's so separate from his own soul's concerns. Now let Ivan stop and go downstairs, out the door and out the sidewalk to check and see if the mail has come. He puts on his hat and wears sunglasses for protection. If there's anything good he'll come back and tell you. He's back, and rather glad to report that indeed mailbox was empty. Enough for one day! The neighborhood kids are home from school. They're shouting and hooting, and that makes the dogs stuck all day in backyards start to bark. Time to hide in the back room and watch the news framed by the TV window.

Jerk

They were in a dark room and could not see each other. The son Josh took a pocketknife out of his pocket and unfolded the blade.

"I heard that," the father said. "That's the blade my father gave me and I gave you."

"I'm tired of it," Josh said. "Always worrying I'll lose it and how furious you'll get."

"That's why I gave it to you. That's what family's all about."

"You made me clean my plate. You said they were starving in China."

"I know what's got your goat," the father replied. "You're mad because I kicked you out of the house because of the drugs you kept doing in your room."

"It's too dark in here," Josh came back. "We need some light. I'm going to open up a wound in you with this blade. Have you forgotten my days in jail when you wouldn't bail me out?"

"Go ahead, jerk that blade around in the dark, Josh. This room's bigger than a basketball court, darker than a coalmine — and yet the world's out there calling, you know, and just in case you've forgotten, it's a fantastical, jocular, magical soup."

Johnny

We walked into this inky black room, closed the door, and now we can't find our way out. Time to make some light. Imagine a twenty-five-year-old Irish woman with flaming red hair lying in bed in a basement apartment on the south side of Chicago. Imagine this beautiful woman Joanna calling her son into her arms and saying, "Now I want you to be good, Johnny. I want you to be good for your foster mother." Imagine I am with Johnny. We have both come from the suburbs where he lives across the street with his foster mother and father. Johnny, my best friend. We are both five years old and it is 1948. Every time I come to Johnny's house I get out the Disney record of Porky Pig and Donald Duck and try to play it, but when Johnny sees me setting the record on the turntable he gets furious and shouts NO. It is spring and I have a rhubarb fight with Johnny in his backyard. We jerk up the rhubarb by their red stems and broad green leaves; we swing them at each other like swords. I always win but this day Johnny gets furious and yells, "I don't want to play," and whacks me in the face and over the head, shredding his rhubarb.

We need more light. Imagine again the beautiful Joanna with red hair lying in the snow-white sheets. I have never seen a woman so beautiful—I know now she looked exactly like the mistress in Dante Gabriel Rossetti paintings, Elizabeth Siddal. It's hard not to become mesmerized and stare at her, but she is tired and must rest. Johnny and I go outside but there are no lawns to play on in front or in back. We each have been given old spoons and go in a narrow space between Johnny's apartment and the one next door, a grey space three feet wide. Johnny just starts digging in the dirt. There we find many small pieces of concrete. We line them up in a row like rocks. "Isn't this fun?" Johnny says. "Isn't this better than where we live?" I am about to say what are you talking about? There are no trees. There are no parks. The cars pass in front of the apartments. It's noisy, it stinks, I am about to say it all, but for the first time a door opens and I glimpse the dim light. I start to awaken. I've been opened, wounded by the world as she is, and begin to sympathize. O Johnny's mom, and O Johnny! Lord, give me words to speak that carry the magic right.

King and Queen

I know you didn't like me, but that's kind of natural for stepmothers. A lot of people don't like me and I take it as a compliment. I try to be a benevolent Queen but perhaps at times I've failed. A ruler cannot appear weak.

This note seems already too much about me. I have not forgotten that you were from a foreign land and may have found adjustment to our country's culture a challenge. I recall your devout faith, and how you pretended to liberal views but were deep down conservative. Still, I loved your laughter, how it would trill out like a song of the loon and fill a room with a crazy mournful sound. I recall you managed to be quite charming during the time you courted my father. Your acting was impressive and as a young girl you succeeded in fooling me. I was happy to see my father happy and did not resent his marrying.

All the work you made me do around the house, while your own daughters lounged or played silly games, taught me discipline and made me strong.

Maybe you did not mind dying alone, did not mind your blood daughters dispersed, married well enough considering their looks, and living far away. Maybe the few priests at your funeral, you felt, were enough to assure you a kind reception in heaven.

I know that even before I was your Queen you were convinced that I was bound for hell. Still, I would have liked to have been informed that you were ill. You needn't have feared me. I would have paid visits and made certain you were as comfortable as possible in your last days.

All I received was a notice of your death from a solicitor, and when I wrote for a small token of our old house — some remembrance of you and my step-sisters and father and mother — the solicitor replied that the church had sent in the auctioneers and sold everything.

The solicitor is soon to learn that the Queen is displeased. The King loves me and we stand together. We have three beautiful young children, although the child bearing has made my feet too large to fit into those old glass slippers.

Both the solicitor and your church will soon learn the extent of the monarchy's distemper.

Sincerely,

Queen Cinderella

Knowing

It's too bad Michelangelo got permission from the Pope to carry out his dissections of human corpses. Or was it Leonardo? Knight can't keep these Italians straight. Anyway, the Popes had seen enough of war to know that the body runs red when the skin is cut or punctured. This could have been water made from the tears of God. This could have been the ambrosia of our souls spurting out. The hands of tiny, invisible angels might have sat by each wound with tiny invisible fans trying to dry the blood to seal and heal the wound. There could have been a variety of birds that lived in our chests on the limbs of our white ribs that would feel called to burst into songs painfully beautiful. Our very urine could have been shuffled off to alchemists in precious vials with the chance of being transformed to gold — or so we might have not known, but believed.

Lifeless as a Park Bench Bum

Leon Trotsky, Lenin's Bolshevik sidekick, exiled to Mexico by Stalin, is leaning over his desk, happy as a clam, correcting a manuscript brought to him by Ramón Mercader, who he considered a friend and supporter, but is likely a Soviet agent sent by Stalin.

Mercader, calm as a cucumber, removes his raincoat with the ice pick inside and sets the raincoat on a nearby table. He is thinking of Raskolnikov from Dostoevsky's novel *Crime and Punishment*, who killed a greedy pawnbroker with a hatchet inside his coat. Raskolnikov had been reading Nietzsche and was beginning to see himself as a superman, above the conventions of law.

Trotsky is so involved with the text in front of his nose that he does not see Ramon take out the ice pick, raise it in the air, and knife him in his skull. Trotsky is a man, whatever his defects, still deeply involved in his work. He is a sophisticated man, in love with modern poetry, a man who once had a short affair with the great Mexican painter Frida Kahlo. Lecherous as a Billy Goat. Lenin and he discussed who first should take the reigns of state power, and Trotsky graciously suggested Lenin because the Russians would never let a Jew be their leader.

Trotsky spits in Ramon's face and fights him till his bodyguards rush in the room. Don't kill him, Trotsky says. He must live to tell the tale. The next day, August

21, 1940, Trotsky lies dead in hospital. O life more fragile than a silver spider web—as fragile as Trotsky.

Lightness of Being

It's pretty astounding, living in a large neighborhood and knowing no names.

I drive up and down these leaf-shadowed streets, past all these houses, so cleanly, so calmly, fiddling with the radio knobs, whistling a loopy tune. The residential streets are perfectly maintained — no cracks or bumps — but the people I have not actually ever met, not shook hands with a single soul.

It's true, I don't have the faintest idea of whom I'd turn to if I were in trouble, so I turn to 911.

But I *do* know the names of two rabbits that live not far from the pond at the park three blocks down. I named them myself — Lola and Laurine. They do not run from me when I sight them nibbling in the fading light. I can't say why, but I find that a lovely consolation.

And also, let me tell you, fences talk and comfort me as they always have. They like to be photographed in the nude, and we understand each other's loneliness.

Just think about it. Beyond these my own doors, I know no human lives, I know no human suffering.

Lucinda

—all through the assassinations of Martin Luther King, Malcolm X, John Kennedy, Robert Kennedy, and John Lennon—from 1964 to 1980—Lucinda was a hippie raging at America, believing in Love.

Love looked like your typical Anglo Jesus—tall, thin, bearded, with long brown hair—when she met him at a Rainbow Gathering in the Gila Wilderness in New Mexico in 1976. (I'm not going to explain here what the Rainbow Gatherings are. Please go to the Web and look it up.)

Everyone in Love's commune had special names like Luck, Luminous, or Lovely. Even if you weren't a member, but were confused, you could go to Love in his teepee and ask him a question. He always had profound and useful answers.

Lucinda asked Love a question at the Rainbow Gathering. I don't remember what it was or what was troubling her. I don't recall Love's answer, but it was a luscious one, a satisfying one. His eyes were gentle; the way he responded radiated concern.

Love's answer made her feel better for longer than a month. She and her old man stopped arguing and they started to love again and sleep in each other's arms.

I suppose now you can see what's coming. I suppose you've guessed that Lucinda and her old man split a year later, after a big fight over whether or not her biker brother could come and live with them.

I suppose you may have surmised that Love himself got into trouble. He became addicted to cocaine and ran up a huge debt that eventually ate up the resources and destroyed the commune he was spiritual leader of.

What you don't know is that Love moved to Chicago and worked as a trader for the American Stock Exchange in order to pay off his large debts. He could have been killed by his dealer if he'd remained in San Francisco. Love cut his long hippie hair, shaved his beard, he put on a suit coat and tie. Love was no dummy; he intelligently gambled on the market and won. He eventually was able to pay off his huge cocaine debts and owns a lovely home in Chicago.

Let me tell you, I've been in apartments where I could hear drug dealers torturing a man who owed them money. The screaming, it's terrible, and can go on all night. I've always been afraid to call the police in such situations. I knew the drug dealers might come for me.

By the way, I'm telling you the truth here. I didn't make a word of this up—and let me add, although I haven't seen Lucinda in ten years, I still believe in Love, whatever he happens to be doing. I hope Love still holds out hope for love in this laboring world, and although lonely now for many years, in my fifties, I am still going to Rainbow Gatherings and still traveling the circuit of Renaissance Festivals selling leather sandals, I dream of someday sleeping in the arms of the one I always loved, Love's former woman, Lucinda. With luck and the Internet I may locate her.

Lucky

Lucky's never been without a place to crash. At times it's been a tent in the woods; at times the back of a station wagon parked off a remote road, but usually he slept well, mattress on the floor, in an ordinary, unadorned room of a large abandoned house or an apartment. You see, he's been mostly lazy, lying around watching movies and television, reading books and writing, barely talking to anyone. The son of a bitter alcoholic, his goal was to get by, not to worry about money or success.

Lucky's never been without a meal. Cans of sardines, bags of potatoes, pinto beans, peanut butter and jelly. He never missed a meal for lack of funds, although it's gotten close. Lucky's done his share of cooking on a camper stove. He's done his share of party crashing and inviting himself over to friends' places. For a couple of months he ran on five-dollar checks arriving daily at a post office box, payment for a collection of short stories he published himself. Another time he made the rent on a large royalty check issued by another firm. Sometimes he'd get busy and forget to eat, but always, whether alone or with family, he usually could look around and find something to rustle out of the refrigerator or off the shelves. Lucky's plucked out aluminum cans from the tall grass walking miles and miles down roadsides that move from wet counties to dry ones, to sell by weight for cash. He's pulled coins out of sofas. Ever made Indian fry bread? It's pretty good.

Yes Lucky has been lazy. He never bought into the American dream. He's watched with disgust and anger those slaves, he calls them, who work forty to sixty hours a week, eight to ten hours a day five or six days a week. Work to die for, work to lie for, work to serve the wealthy dreams of those they'll never meet. Lucky has hated these thieves and murderers, out like termites to bite away our lives hour by hour by hour, out to steal our liberty and pursuit of happiness. Still, his anger never cut him off from the bounty of the land. Months passed when the only money he had was the bills folded in the back pocket of his pants. Yet always Lucky's been fed and clothed. Always Lucky's found a place and found love.

Lucky To Be

Pardon the confusion here, the words spilling out in no prefabricated order. Laird lays no claim to knowing what he's talking about, but let him run on about being in and around San Francisco's great bookstore—the store founded by the populist poet Lawrence Ferlinghetti, City Lights Bookstore—when Laird was forty-five years old in 1988 and had quit the bookstore business himself. He's thinking about it twenty years later, and while Laird thinks, Ferlinghetti—that old anarchist—is still kicking around town, painting and writing, ninety-four years young.

Laird can see him in his mind as an intense young man, in a lost National Educational Television eight-millimeter black and white film, reciting long surrealist poems, jumping from shade to sunlight, face behind a celluloid mask, up on the roof of his bookstore in the 1950's. In 1988 Laird was near the front of the store, when a woman rushed up asking for help to get her car unlocked, and he refused, wondering if it was some kind of scam, and advised her to call the police. Laird did not come to San Francisco from Texas to spend his one free day trying to search for a coat hanger to undo a door. No, he was looking for unusual books—books with ideas not easily come by in the South that might unlock keys to the universe.

Then a young man in his twenties went in and tried to get the clerk behind the counter, his "friend," to loan him fifty dollars. The man kept begging and begging, and the clerk kept shrugging his shoulders and saying no and no. For the ten years Laird ran his bookstore in Austin, no one came to the counter to beg for money.

A great blue December San Francisco day it was. The whitecaps out in the bay were sure to have been singing Handel's Hallelujah Chorus.

Earlier, one sailor at Vesuvio's Bar next door, across what is now the tiny Jack Kerouac Street, had tried to trade sex with an older man for cocaine. The two saw Laird studying them in the bar mirror and the younger one shouted, "Hey, what do you want, cunt face?" Laird was bigger than both of them—and the bartender winked to signal he was on Laird's side—so he took his time and finished his Anchor Steam Beer—rated by many, by the way, the greatest American beer and made in San Francisco.

Earlier Laird had been inside the great City Lights Bookstore, as mentioned, and been down the stairs in the basement, sitting in a chair looking over magazines, and then he practiced a little anarchy himself, slipping copies of his own books that he was carrying in his backpack onto various shelves, only to receive, a year later, a letter of effusive praise from a man he's never met but still corresponds with. He has remained Laird's greatest fan.

Then Laird went back upstairs to the front, as mentioned, and the last thing he noticed was a line of tense young women forming in front of the store where the big windows are. They were dressed conservatively, as if they worked in one of the many office buildings nearby, such as the Transamerica Pyramid, and Laird could read a hunger in the stiffness of their limbs, and one by one the women went off with men in dark suits, and being alone, he almost wished he were a man in a dark suit, and not a cunt-faced stranger from Texas in jeans and a sweatshirt, so he could pick up someone beautiful and smart, but then he understood why the extreme tenseness and impatience, when he caught a look in their eyes. It was fifteen after five, and they were out there hoping to trade sex for heroin—or for a quick influx of cash to buy heroin. Laird turned and looked at Ferlinghetti's paintings high on the walls of the bookshop and shouted, "O AMERICA, HOW I LOVE YOUR PAIN OF FREEDOM!"

It's amazing what you can get away with in stores, because the customer is always right. A few folks looked up from books, but when Laird did nothing more they returned to reading and browsing.

All his life Laird's done well with the pain of freedom. He's been happy, but could have used more freedom. How is it with you? Still, Laird wonders how those women are doing. It had to be heroin they were after, don't you think, or maybe amphetamines? But aren't amphetamines cheap? What can Laird say? Deep down he's content, lucky to be a small town boy from Texas.

Man

I used to nestle at my mother's nipple—but that's beyond my memory. I do recall sucking my thumb and hugging my security blanket. My mother would paint bitter liquid on my thumb to stop my sucking, but it didn't work. Later I had a Teddy bear my father slipped under my arm each night after reading me a story. The bear would grow in my mind to protect me from terrifying monsters under the bed and in the closet that often woke me cold and shivering in the middle of the night.

I keep a pistol under my pillow now. I put its cold comfort against my lonely cheek at times. I put its muzzle between my lips. The gun helps me feel secure in the dark. I've never used it for hunting. It protects me from a world I do not know and will never understand. I know this gun to be a reliable friend, and it will take me from myself if and when I'm ready.

Mirror Lipstick

Tonight, as soon as Milton gets home, he is going to write a poem on the bathroom mirror with lipstick. Yes, he'll be writing on a mirror with red lipstick for the first time, looking into his own eyes, and noticing the wrinkles and blemishes on his face. He is wondering if this will make for a kind of honesty. Is it not what women do when they are leaving their lovers? They write their truth, what they've been holding in, in a place that the lover cannot miss, that will obstruct for a moment his vision of himself. As they leave, with tears moving in the corners of their eyes, they will at last be getting through to him. Has Milton imagined a scene that does not exist? Has he imagined a scene in a movie that perhaps someday he will repeat? Hopefully not. His daughter has written messages on the bathroom mirror when she's had friends over and they were doing each other's hair. Milton can't remember a single one of these messages, but he does remember trying, with some irritation, various means to get the messages off. *Nosce te ipsum* — he doesn't know how to pronounce it — but it means in Latin "know thyself." "Know thyself" could mean knowing your limits, knowing your divinity, knowing yourself psychologically, and a host of other things. Red lipstick making words on a mirror — he wonders how hard you have to mash. Can you write in script or only in print? Perhaps the mirror might mumble what to write. He could write that I will love you, even beyond our mortal end. He could write that for his wife and in that forever moment believe.

Miss Lonely Heart

grew up in an orphanage in Milton, Mississippi, and as often happens with people brought up in orphanages, she never mastered social skills and lacked all her life much human contact. She lived deep in the Mississippi woods, grew her own garden, kept pigs and chickens, and was able to manage a living off her syndicated newspaper column. She was fond of her animals and garden plants, and often wept at the dinner table when eating these companions in order to survive. She felt like a general ordering troops into battle and certain death for the benefit of their country. Her body was her country. And Miss Lonely Heart knew loneliness inside out, upside down, and all the way through, and through her many years managed to give a fair amount of beneficial advice to her readers. I had long been lonely and an avid fan of her column. I got to visit her one morning in May when flowers were blooming around her cottage everywhere. A newspaper gave me the address.

"You know," she said, "there's no reason to be lonely, what with a world full of things that are lonely too and crying out for a friend. Take this fork, for instance. We have been quite intimate, three times a day, some twenty-five years. The tines of the fork have a kind of humming music that daily softly sings to me. They will praise—half seriously of course—the warm cave of my mouth that they have penetrated so many times to keep me fed and alive."

"Young man," she added as I was leaving, "be a master of your heart."

Moodist

Molly hates her life. She's stuck in a fundamentalist town with more peroxide blondes per square inch than Palm Beach, Florida. She loves her life. Some drunken college kids passing by in the middle of the night ripped up her backyard fence. They didn't know she was the women's state wrestling champ of Ohio. She caught them and beat them up, took their driver's licenses, and told them they'd better bring their asses back the next morning to fix the fence. Molly hates her life. Her teeth are good. Her health is good. Her one kid remaining at home gets good grades in school. Her husband never complains about the messy house, the messy yard, her remodeling projects not completed. Molly loves her life. She doesn't have money. She can't afford home insurance. She can't sleep at night. Her memory's going bad. Molly hates her life. She has two grandchildren. Her house is paid for. She has no debts. Her husband tells at least one good joke a day. She and her dog are the wisdom figures. This is the way it is and the way it's supposed to be. She loves, she hates, her life.

Mother was Randy

Why did Monty's mother not die earlier? This was the question Monty asked Gog monthly.

"If you exist, Gog," Monty asked, "why did you not take my mother sooner?"

Mother did nothing for forty years. Dad paid her two thousand a month in alimony. She lived by herself for thirty years in one room in a Geriatric Center in West Texas. She had no friends; she watched television all day while stretched out on her back in bed. Her favorite thing to watch was NCAA basketball. She loved to watch the athletic men run around in flashy shorts.

"Gog, why did you not take my mother earlier? Why did you wait until she was 84, ten years after my dad passed away? Dad worked hard to support the family and put his kids through college. He paid sister's therapy bills for twenty years. He did research to find a cure for heart disease.

"Perhaps it was not you, Gog, who took her?" She complained of pain in her arms and shoulders. Monty felt her arm and moved her shoulder one day as she lay in bed. Apparently her bones were so fragile Monty broke something.

An ambulance took her to the hospital. Monty rushed after the ambulance to visit her; Monty came once a day to see her. When Monty put his hands on her head she opened her eyes, but she made no movement and mouthed no words. She'd had a stroke a decade earlier in a dentist chair while getting her teeth removed. She could not speak.

Gog, did Monty inadvertently kill his own mother?

Why do you not punish Monty, Gog?

So many children die of cancer — Monty's been to the pediatric wards with his nurse friend Moira. Those children, they tear you up inside, they are so knowing and accepting of their fates, Gog.

Gog, you could have saved one of those children and might have taken Monty's mother.

As mentioned, Monty's mother liked to watch basketball. She said watching the men run up and down the courts in their shorts turned her on. Maybe you saved her, Gog, because you admired her honesty, her randy spirit.

My Former Beloved,

who lives in poverty on a piece of land in remote mountains, exactly as she told me she would do thirty years ago, in a small trailer provided by her mother, over ninety years old. O my once beloved, after recent numerous small strokes, cared for now by her single mother daughter working for Girling Health. She, Myrna, my ex-wife, wrote me recently to get my social security number, so as to get higher social security payments herself. She did not believe I would send her the number, out of meanness, I suppose. Before her strokes she'd have known that number — she never needed to look up the addresses of my relatives she'd never met to mail them Christmas cards each year.

I am lying in bed with insomnia this late October morning. Myrna came to mind as she sometimes does around Halloween. After all we were married twenty years.

Ah my former, she lived after we split on the college streets of Boulder, sleeping in bushes. I learned so much from her very human paradoxes, learned how when we were poor I took the pressures of poverty better than she, by making it a badge of macho pride, while she, she merely refused to get a decent job, keeping to the Indian attitude that working for any other human was slavery. My dear former, she with her infectious charismatic optimism and droves of friends who have now disappeared in her remoteness, she who hummed happy tunes throughout the day as we worked together in our small bakery, she who was, surprisingly, born with a darker soul than I, imagining me once her murderer, capable of pushing her off the roof of the house where we were repairing shingles. I won't shadow your legacy by a lengthy bill of particulars, my former beloved, nor will I ponder long the long list of consolations you grasped, my military brat, child of a lieutenant colonel, attending five high schools and never living in a place long enough to get from the soul of the soil any sense of value.

Those consolations — the marijuana, when younger the LSD, the Pentecostal Church, the Neopaganism, the belief in Tarot, I Ching, astrology, alternative health, and the magic power of hot springs — while I stumbled amiably along in my family's moralistic liberal Midwestern Unitarian-Universalism, in my naïve, built-in, unquestioning trust in the possibilities of goodness for all humankind, always disappointed, always shocked and cynical while she, she bravely struggled to maintain hope, always seeking the silver threads in the dark, and then her hopes would be dashed. One son living in an abandoned trailer he salvaged alongside a highway now on the same land as hers, an alcoholic on disability with AIDS; another son a cocaine regular spinning records in a Boulder strip bar, and her former speedster daughter, so sweet, now caring for her, raising a son too. It's the six of you, my former and her three children and two grandchildren, a family that holds together. Is it fair to say she cut one wing on each of her children, so they might never be able to fly from the nest?

Former beloved, genius writer, she who has survived the death of a first husband and the death of a long-term lover when after me she gave up on the idea of marriage, I miss your cheery optimism, I miss your light around and darkness you unconsciously generated, my *bruja* struggling to be a *curandera*. Who can know another person? What I have written is accurate and unfair. I'm selfish I know, but some moments I miss how we moved through the ruby dark chaos of all those years, my eyes on the sky's bright utopian constellations, oblivious, so in love.

My Room

My room, it has asked that I not describe itself to you. It is a room after all. It was made and exists in service of privacy. It's been irritated lately. I've ignored my room's requests that I lock the door, that I put a "Do Not Disturb" sign on the door. I only keep a hatchet in a corner. My room wants me to tell you that the blinds are always closed, that the view out its single, small high window faces a brick wall.

It will neither deny nor confirm that there is a bed. It most certainly refuses to comment on what people, if any, might sleep in the bed, and it won't confirm or deny, nor will it comment on any love that may or may not fleet through its spaces. It will not comment on any possible job, happiness, sorrow, or grieving. As to the existence of a writing desk, or a plasma television, the room does not feel qualified to address such matters. It lays no claim to know much about art or entertainment.

What is it most proud of?

The silence it makes. The solitude it keeps.

Narrative

Although Nadia no longer loves me, I try to grow and can as many fruits and vegetables as possible. Although my vegetables are not grown organically, the Rio Grande Chirping frog has expanded its range into East Texas nearly as far north as Tyler. Although the Rio Grande Chirping frogs make a novel squeak at dusk from suburban flowerbeds, the stock market continues to vacillate erratically up and down while tending up. Although the stock market this week dropped its deepest drop—seven hundred points—a bird somehow got trapped in my chimney, died, and stunk up the house with a nasty fishy smell. Although flies were drawn inside in droves by the nasty smell, banks all over the world are in recovery. Although failing banks often get nationalized, a tree died in my front yard. Although Nadia has not taken down the tree yet, there has been no shortage of gas to purchase at nearby pumps at high prices. Although Nadia never tries to cut back on gas, McDonalds is now selling an Asian salad and fancy coffee to upgrade its image. Although their coffee's too sweet and their Asian salad is full of fattening cheese, I don't seem to be able to stop making the reader nod off, using my prose poems often as cannons to shoot out words that half deconstruct meaning. Although meaning gets thrown around inside these poems like a tossed salad, a woman still weeps gathering nasturtiums from the Queen's garden at Buckingham Palace. Although that woman—Nadia—no longer loves me, the nasturtiums continue to bloom, the petals continue to fall.

Nature

You find a day when no wind stirs the autumn of trees. You find a temperature when you no longer mark the progress of the sun through the blazing sky. You find a place where there are no people and no sounds but the movement of your clothes where you sit. A pure lake lies before you like a near perfect mirror. Perhaps after a while you pick up the trickle of water or a farm dog barking lazily in the distance.

Now in the solitude you can believe for a moment that time is not passing. Everything seems so blessedly still. You're enjoying the colors in the high grass around you and do not notice the beat of your own heart. Ah quiet, ah stillness, ah astonishment, the reality you hold in the moment, that you are not mortal.

Nature Hike

Naomi's here now in this fiction to take you up the Little Brazos River—no Fiction in history has taken a group up the Little Brazos River, a tributary off the regular Brazos in Texas. We're doing it in mid-September. We drive down a narrow road and park under the bridge for State Highway 21 that passes high over the river.

Once down in the cool flowing water, Naomi, wearing rubber boots to keep the wetness off, starts seining with another adventurer. The seining net keeps coming up with nothing. The water has cut through a black strip of soft rock, this layer left over from the dust stirred up when a large meteor struck in the Yucatan, or is it when a large volcano exploded the Yucatan? Naomi can't remember and neither can the Fiction. The dust was packed into soft stone and nurtured well the cotton fields of the slave plantations in this river bottom area. The carbon dust fell on the land twenty million years ago.

This is a nature trip, but Naomi is more interested in a graffiti style mural sprayed on the strut from an old collapsed railroad bridge. The Fiction wishes it were a camera to take pictures of the mural. The mural seems to be the celebration of the heroism of soldiers in the current Iraqi war.

Why would an artist wade up the Little Brazos with his cans of spray paint to spray paint a mural that no one will see? Fiction asks Naomi. Why did prehistoric man need to paint in caves? These are the kinds of questions Fiction loves to speculate on but do not interest much Naomi. Maybe audience does not matter, or maybe your audience is an occasional initiate who arrives once a year. At least in this remote place no one will try to destroy the mural. Naomi wishes, for no more than a second, that she were a mural painted on the old concrete buttresses of a collapsed railroad bridge up the Little Brazos River.

Never Dreamed

Neva went camping. Why tell you where? Actually Neva doesn't remember where, but she could find a map and figure it out. Somewhere in north central Texas she pulled into this campsite around eleven at night in one of the few remaining spots.

Her plan was to sleep on the rubber mat she'd thrown in the back of her pickup. It was too late and too dark and too chilled to get out and try to put up the tent. Ten minutes after she'd climbed inside her sleeping bag, Neva woke to hear a banging on her truck. She got her flashlight out and shined it into a constellation of golden orbs. What a sight! As her eyes adjusted Neva began to catch sight of their bodies. They looked in silhouette like monkeys. And then not ten feet away, on the hood, she saw one, an albino, an albino raccoon, totally white with the same golden orbs, like a cat's, staring her way with a curious face, for a long moment, before leaping off and leaping up into a large dumpster not twenty feet away.

Neva could have given up and gotten in her truck and driven to a nearby motel, but what's one lost night's sleep next to what you've never dreamed of, what you are graciously given and will never see again?

No Funny Business

Noah and Nan are sitting in a booth together upstairs in Austin's Deep Eddy Tavern, sharing pitchers of beer and complaining about their jobs.

Noah drives for Yellow Cab and has a thousand stories of the nuts that rode with him. "The worst," he says, "is when a transvestite picks up a straight guy and the guy starts trying to noodle in the back seat and figures out his she is a he."

Nan works for an answering service and also has a collection of strange uplifting tales. "People will call me and ask how to get the Norway rats out of their attics," she laughs. "I tell them this is an answering service and we've got all the answers. I'll be glad to come over and do the job for five hundred bucks."

They're both drunks, and for the last couple of months have been bumping into each other at Deep Eddy Tavern most nights. Sometimes they talk; mostly they don't. Nan sits with the women drunks and Noah hobnobs with the men. But now it's closing time so Noah invites Nan down to his apartment in the basement for more talk and beers.

"That's sounds great to me," she says, "as long as there ain't no funny stuff."

"What? You're telling me I can't make a joke in my own apartment," Noah quips.

They have to walk out the front door of the tavern, where a year ago the previous owner had been shot and killed by an irate customer, and then walk downhill to the back of the building where the door to the basement apartment hides nearly behind a bush.

"Ever go swimming at Deep Eddy Pool down the way?" Nan asks Noah.

"No," he says, "and as a matter of fact, the two years I've lived here I've never been down to check it out."

"They got some big trees along the Colorado. I used to bring my daughter when she was young, before I lost custody."

"I'm sorry," Noah says.

"It was a good thing, I realized in the end," she continues. "I was a mess; I'm still a mess but not the mess I was then."

Noah unlocks the door, flips the switch, and they go inside. "All I've got is one six pack," he says, opening the door to his small refrigerator.

"I don't use birth control," Nan says, "so if you try the funny stuff and I give in you might end up a proud daddy."

"That's good to know," Noah says.

The oil based white paint on the four walls of the one-room efficiency has turned yellow. The floor of the efficiency apartment is cement and pipes nest along the low ceiling.

"I bet you got a lot of roaches down here, so close to the river," Nan says. She takes the only chair in the place, a dirty blue sofa chair, about three feet from the bed. She sits so her feet are tucked under and the roaches can't nibble on her legs. "You could get a couple of those chemical foggers and bomb them out."

"I don't believe in chemical warfare," Noah replies. "The only good thing Nixon did was plow under the chemical and biological weapons."

"Don't the roaches bother you at night?" Nan asks.

"They entertain me; they're less trouble than most people." Noah goes to his closet and gets his pistol. "The rule is you can't shoot at the cement floor or the ceiling. If you shoot the floor the bullet could ricochet and kill us. If you shoot the ceiling it might ricochet off a pipe and kill us or go through the ceiling and kill a customer upstairs. The tavern needs all the drunks it can net, so I only allow shooting at the roaches on the plaster walls." Noah hands the pistol to Nan.

"You know, I like this game. I like it because we're bound to fail. We're drunk. How can we hit a tiny spot on the wall?"

"You're right, but it's fun to try. Look to the left of the fridge. There's a whole batch of them together."

"True, but we're still bound to miss, like we've done all our lives."

"Well, I like to see a few holes in honor of the destruction done to others," Noah says. "Then we can lie down together and hold one another. It'll be like a prayer."

"Come on," Nan says. "I told you no funny business."

"It's not funny," Noah said. "We keep our clothes on. We hug each other tight and try to remember what it was like when we were in love."

"No funny business?"

"That's right. I'll be thinking of my ex-wife, the only woman I ever loved, and all the times she said she would leave cause I drank. Then I'll be remembering the night she finally did walk out with our boys, right down the way at the married student housing when I was working on my Botany PhD. In a little while I'll be crying."

"Now don't get sad on me," Nan says. "You'll ruin our date—and when are you going to get out the beers? How do I aim this thing? It's so heavy.

"I'll get the beers after we shoot. Use both hands. Here, let me get behind you and help."

"How many women have you used this routine on? I see lots of holes in the walls."

"Not many."

"You're lucky no one's shot you instead of the roaches."

"I never have much to drink around, plus, well, they still want to believe in love."

Normal

You have no idea, until you've been around them, how normal normal people can be. The normal don't care how late it is, or if the last room in the house is burning, they are smiling, they haven't forgotten to say thank you, and not for once have they stopped believing in our legal system or in our heroes.

Do they imagine their reward in heaven to be infinite shelves at Nordstrom's? They will be rewarded in a new timeless world with no limit on their credit cards. Does Jesus drive around heaven tanned in a new red Mustang with the top down, his halo blowing Bach fugues in the natty wind?

Ah the normal people, God bless them, so busy smiling, saying thank you, and checking faces in the mirrors. They remind Norman of garbanzo beans in a can. They remind Norman of the shag in 1970's brown and yellow cheap motel carpets. How much work it takes to be normal, or is it easy and instinctual? Norman doesn't know, but he does know they have no time for questions.

Not to Talk About

The stethoscope hangs like a black noose in his daughter's closet. Years ago she would listen to his heart, he would listen to her heart. Their hearts would tick mortally, mutually. At times they'd put the stethoscope against a wall and see if they could hear others talking on the other side. They were spies giggling together, Norman and his daughter Natalie.

Norman remembers the moment he explained to Natalie how the stethoscope worked and how her eyes grew large with rapt attention.

The black stethoscope belonged to her grandmother the doctor, one of three who graduated from medical school at the University of Minnesota during World War II. Grandmother is now eighty-two and paralyzed so she can't move or talk. She lies in a nursing home thirty minutes north of where they live.

Norman has never told his daughter, who is now seventeen and listens rarely to what he has to say, that his mother quit her medical practice to stay at home. He doesn't tell his daughter how the stethoscope lay in a drawer in his parent's bedroom for twenty years. He doesn't say how his mother used her medical license to order sleeping pills since she stayed at home and rarely saw anybody, or how his mother attempted suicide twice in a great manipulative cry for attention by swallowing gobs of those sleeping pills.

Norman doesn't say that he has only one of his

mother's remaining things, this stethoscope that hangs like a black noose in the closet.

Now You Know. Now You Know How it is.

Nolan's girlfriend — get this — keeps asking Nolan to take her back to his place.

"Aren't you rushing things, Nolan says? You may be twenty-seven but I'm nineteen. We do have a good time, don't we?"

They walk up and down the Strand, enjoy the sea air and go into stores like Colonel Bubbies, where they sell new and old military surplus equipment from all over the world.

Nolan's girlfriend knows his dad was in Vietnam and that Nolan's interested in military equipment and uniforms. She buys him a beret from the Norwegian Army. They visit the art galleries and fancy dress shops she likes. At night they go into the upscale bars where his girl — Norma's her name — orders a glass or two of house white and Nolan sneaks his share of sips.

"You've been to my place," Norma says. She works at Sealy Hospital as a copy editor for a medical magazine and lives in a garage apartment in the neighborhood. "You've been in my bed," she adds, curling a smile on her lips and turning her head slightly. "Why can't I be in yours?"

"You know I live at home," Nolan lies for the nineteenth time. "You know I haven't moved out, for financial reasons. What's the rush anyway? We've known each other just two months? My mom and dad are cool but they're not so cool they'd let me bring a girl home to bed."

"There's nothing wrong with my meeting your parents, is there?" she asks.

They've had this conversation forty times. "You are nine years older," Nolan mentions again, gently. "An English teacher — I could have been in your class."

What Nolan doesn't dare tell her is he doesn't have an actual place to stay. He belongs to a gym where he showers, but he doesn't have a regular job.

Nolan figures he could say he lives by his wits. He works part-time sticking advertising fliers in people's doors for steady cash.

Norma thinks he's a freshmen at the A&M campus in Galveston. I guess you could say I am a student, a student of life, Nolan thinks to himself. He moved down from Dallas and has been in Galveston a year. Norma and Nolan met in the Rosenberg Library on a rainy April Sunday. He was reading a book of Philip Caputo stories on Vietnam. He read a lot on Vietnam since his father died a year ago of complications, at forty-four, from exposure to Agent Orange. His mother's drinking got worse, and he left when he couldn't get her to stop.

Norma was reading *The New Yorker* magazine. He liked the way her turquoise eyes peeked out from her thick bangs of brown hair, and asked if she read the articles or enjoyed the cartoons.

Norma says early on a Saturday night while they're listening to a bad Austin band in a club off the Strand, says with a tear running down her cheek that she won't be seeing Nolan again after this cloudless June night, unless he takes her home to meet his mother and father. She says he needs to be more open about his life, that if he loves her he can't be afraid of age differences.

And so Norma and Nolan catch the green trolley to the Seawall, they ride down the Seawall north till they get where there are few stores and hotels. It is still light and the evening is cool enough with a sea breeze blowing. He takes her hand and they walk out on the sand through the brush and then around a hill. He gets his flashlight out of his backpack and leads her through a cement doorframe inside an old World War II bunker. "You know how I am interested in war," Nolan is explaining to her.

The bunker smells of mold and salt and damp, but to Nolan it's not that unpleasant.

"They were worried about an invasion by the Axis powers by sea, and so the government built three of these bunkers on the island," he says, "and they're still here. Isn't it amazing? Here it is 1984 and these bunkers must be forty years old. You can see in the floor (he shines the light) where the big artillery could rotate. The big guns pointed through this large horizontal slit here out to sea. Behind some of these steel doors they kept the ammo."

Norma is mostly quiet. She does say the place is not romantic like the beach where they often take walks at night. She asks if he is thinking of enlisting in the military and he says no way, they already got my father.

"Over here is where the soldiers lived," he adds. Nolan pulls down on a big latch on a steel door and pushes the heavy rusted door open.

"This is where I stay." He shines the light inside. "I've got three suitcases full of clothes, a sleeping bag, a pillow, and a foam rubber mat. I've got an old pistol for protection but it's so dark in here I never get bothered."

Norma doesn't say a word. Nolan can't make out her face, but he is thinking how much he loves her, that she is his first love and he will love her till he dies. At nineteen he does not care much for the world. He has no plans beyond enjoying the freedom of the day to day. Deep inside the bunker they can hear the trickle of water.

Norma is still holding his hand. She gives it a squeeze and puts her other hand over his hand too and gives a sigh. He hears a sniffle and surmises she might be crying again, or maybe it's the sound of water dripping.

After a long moment standing there with the flashlight lighting his home and belongings, Norma says quietly, "Can we go?"

"Now you know," Nolan says. "Now you know how it is."

On Justice

It's possible that zombies who have been murdered can locate a private company that has developed a spaceship to approach the speed of light. At least the millionaire zombies can locate such a company.

As their corporate craft approaches light speed, time slows down for the zombies while the earth speedily spins. The relative effect, when they return to earth, will be that zombies have gone back in time.

How far back in time? That detail of the mystery is not yet understood. They may be highly fortunate and walk off the runway of the corporate craft young and alive again, at a time before they died or were murdered, with the knowledge to prevent any murder. They may be rich again—such are the marvels of modern science!

If however they are less fortunate, and arrive back on earth after they died or were murdered, they yet arrive at a time closer to the event, and can become detectives determined to solve the crime or disease that led to their demise. Was it Professor Plum or Miss Scarlet Fever? Did it happen in the conservatory with a lead pipe or in the study with a virus? Zombies as they are, they will have plenty of time to examine every box of clues, above ground and under.

A third benefit will be the re-socialization of at least some zombies as useful citizens. No longer will they be walking out of fog in the woods in large mobs, ready to engage in the most brutal violence. Once they have solved the crime of their own demise they can go on to take on other cases.

Eventually many bright zombies who were unable to recover their fortunes — because wills are legal contracts and must be honored — will rise to high ranks in law enforcement and the justice system. In fact, many have already, sitting on some of the highest courts of the land.

Order of the Sweaty Palms

Her entire life, since adolescence, was dominated by sweaty palms. What boy wants to dance with a girl with sweaty palms? Orpha smeared on many brands of deodorants. In 1959 Arid Extra Dry didn't even make a dent in her tropical rain forest. Her mother talked to a surgeon about removing the sweat glands, but the surgeon said it would leave her hands scarred and grooved.

Orpha couldn't even stand to hold hands with herself. She'd pick up an object and leave sweat or a stain behind. She'd been told it was all anxiety—all in her head. She'd been told to think about cold mountain lakes, or to meditate, concentrating on her breath, the slow breathing in and out of life.

All because of her hands Orpha knew her hair to be mouse brown instead of dirty blonde, she knew her face was heavily pocked by acne scars that no foundation could ever hide, she knew her breasts too small and her hips too wide. She spent a fortune on gloves at Macy's and at various therapists' offices. The message they taught was loud and clear: it was all because of her sweaty hands that no one would ever love her and she'd die alone and childless in a room.

"I have these terrible sweaty hands, and so I say, screw God," she told the priest in the confession booth early one evening. She had been drinking all afternoon at a tavern downtown, hoping some man would make a move on her, and her face was red with anger.

"My child," said the priest from the other side of the booth where she could not see him. "Calm down. Palm Sunday is coming. Marry Jesus; become a nun. You'll get none, but you'll have a man, and Jesus, having his own palm problems, easily forgives sweaty palms."

Orpha took the priest's advice and became a nun. She learned quickly that she was not the only nun with sweaty palms. When she sat in the lounge with the others smoking cigarettes and Mother Superior wasn't around, they called themselves The Order of Sweaty Palms.

Out By Munson Creek

"Give me my blowgun," Otis said.

Orlando handed him the blowgun from the floor on his side. It was dark and cool and they were on a county road sixty miles east of Dallas. The sky was autumn clear; a quarter moon hung low on the horizon.

"You can't drink beer, drive, and shoot that blowgun," I said from the back seat.

"What are you going to shoot?" Orlando asked.

"I don't know. Maybe you," said Otis.

"Fuck," said Orlando.

"Fuck you," said Otis.

"You got poison?" I asked.

"Sure," Otis said. "Hand me the box. It's under the seat."

"Shit," I said. "I'm too drunk." I found the plastic box. After a bit of a struggle I got the lid open and handed Otis a dart over his shoulder. Minutes before we got to the bridge at Munson Creek, Otis handed me the blowgun.

"You load it," he said.

I took the blowgun and realized it was merely PVC pipe. It had a rubber mouthpiece at one end. I put a dart in from that end, not sure what I was doing. "Where'd you get this?" I asked, "at Canton First Monday or a garage sale or something?"

"I ordered it out of the back of *Soldier of Fortune*," Otis said as we bumped over the narrow wooden bridge. "It's better than a gun. Zip and they're dead. No sound."

"Let's stop and shoot something," Orlando said.

Otis pulled off to the side beyond the bridge.

"You gonna shoot some fish?" I joked.

"Hell no!"

"You can't kill a turtle with that," I added.

"Turtle my eye," Otis said.

"We got to find something to kill," said Orlando.

"That's what we'll do," said Otis. "There's always something around to kill."

We all got out of the car. I could see a few old refrigerators stuck out of Munson Creek where people had shoved them out of their pickups off the bridge.

"All you'll find around here is cows," I said.

"Cows'll do," Orlando added.

"Zip-a-dee-doo-dah," said Otis. "My oh my what a wonderful night."

"Save 'em the long ride to the slaughter house," said Orlando.

"Aren't they milk cows out this way?" I said.

"You country boys know about hunting?" Otis queried.

"No," I said. "We're small town boys. The only thing I know I got from listening to the good ol' boys drinking coffee down at the Dairy Queen on Highway 80."

"Cows should be hunted," Orlando quipped.

"Yeah. It's in their blood, and tonight we're tribesmen."

"Uga booga," I said.

"There's a cow over there," Orlando said.

"Naw, you fuck, that's a log," said Otis.

"I bet you can't even hit that freaking log with that

107

thing," said Orlando.

"What'll you bet me?" said Otis.

"I'll bet you the case I got in my trunk back at the house," I said.

"Naw, that's stupid," said Otis.

"It's dark as shit out here," said Orlando.

"You step in a cow pie?" I asked.

"What about shrooms?" Orlando said. "We could get us some shrooms right out of the cow pies."

"Naw," I said. "They put stuff in the feed. No shrooms anymore and no Kickapoo Joy Juice."

"Get over there," Otis said to me. "I'll shoot you in the leg. You won't hardly feel a thing—sorta like a flu shot."

"Do it," said Orlando.

"No way," I said. "You got poison on those darts."

"Did you bring the box of darts?" Otis asked.

"Orlando did," I said.

"Fuck that, man. You had them in the back seat."

"Fuck. I want to go to war," said Otis. "This is shit. Nothing to do but get drunk or do drugs. I want to go to war."

"I did Desert Storm, man," I said. "Let me tell you, you don't want any of that crap."

"Fuck yeah, man. That's why I joined the reserves," Orlando shot back. "I want to drink and defend my country. I'm ready to ship right now."

"My feet are covered with mud," I said. "The stars are cool out here but let's go back."

"Let me shoot something. Please," said Otis. "Then we can go."

Outgunned

For PL

They all thought him darkly handsome before she came along with those eyebrows out of the dance bands of the 1940's.

A bit wide at the waist that made for crowding at the table, but her eyes—ah her eyes!—they put people on Greek islands enjoying the chalky blue of the Mediterranean.

O how could Owen compete, a mere monkey taught to be silent in his rocky Gibraltar home, while she, all those tropical birds that took their colored turns in her hair, and the mystery of the languages they sang in sudden silver showers out of her lips?

Perfectibility

Everyone's well aware that robots are a lot easier to get along with than humans. They do break down occasionally, but all you need to do is call a repairman to pick your baby up and get her going in a few days.

What these programmers can do is amazing. The first big breakthrough happened after the new millennium when they trained these machines to meet your eyes, look away, and then look up again. It was a bit creepy at first, but one adapts quickly. The dog models seem like real dogs, and the humans seem human. They've also got them built now so you can set your model to a range of feelings. "Agreeable" is of course my favorite setting. I set her there when I want to have sex or when I want her to spend the day cleaning house, cooking a large meal for guests, and doing the laundry.

I myself own the deluxe model. Agreeable is great, but can get a little boring. I like to set my girl on intellectual so we can discuss, in a friendly way, perhaps feminism or post-post modernism. I learn a lot from baby that way. Her memory capacity is astounding. When I ask her, she can always give me the date and time. I can dial her politics knob from fundamentalist conservative through corporate conservative to pragmatic moderate to flaming liberal—and even on to right wing libertarian or left wing nonviolent anarchist.

The features that come with the model are amazing, and can be mixed. If I set her politics knob to, say, fundamentalist conservative, there's a mood knob I can turn so she can come over as angry, dismissive, mean spirited, and even rational. I rarely turn to rational however because baby is so sexy when she's angry. Man it turns me on. "How are you feeling, baby?" I can ask. She will reply, "I am very angry. I don't think I like you right now."

All models come with a remote, just like your TV, so to avoid trouble or damage to her circuitry, I usually switch baby off after she says she may not like me. Sometimes she freezes midsentence, with her hand extended not in a fist but petulantly. She will have the cutest pout. Then I go over and change her settings to "agreeable" and "happy" and fire her up again.

Another feature I like about my model is that she came with accessories. I have a closet full of them. I can quickly change her hairstyle and hair color, her boob size, hip size, the size of her feet, and the color of her eyes. Since her skin is made of stretchable vinyl I can make her pleasingly plump or nail thin like the model Twiggy. This way, to quote Shakespeare on Cleopatra, "Age cannot wither her, nor custom stale her infinite variety." She comes of course with some necklaces I can clip on, and magnetic earrings—much of this stuff is color coordinated. I can buy online more jewelry, clothes, and accessories. There's a button hidden in her nose I can push and she will ask, "How do I look, darling?" Her facial expression will take on a touch of insecurity.

"You look fabulous," I say. "You always look great, baby." I don't tell her that I dressed her. There's probably a block in the programming so she wouldn't receive that message, but I don't want to upset my baby.

I myself was raised Unitarian, and I keep baby's button there nearly all the time so that our world views are the same. But she comes with buttons for Presbyterian, Church of Christ, Jewish, Moslem, Hindu, atheist—you name it. I sure love my baby, and the manufacturer Hasbro sure has come a long way since the old "Barbie" days. I am looking forward to further developments, such as long lasting yet portable internal batteries that will allow us to go on long plane flights together, and a waterproof model so she can show off her figure at the beach. It would be fun if I could alter her skin color and ethnicity, make her Laotian one-day, and Australian aborigine on another. It would be great too if they could get the cost of the deluxe model down to around what today a typical American wedding costs.

Poor Prose Poem

It's lonely inside the shoebox of paragraphs that is the prose poem. We live in the back of closets primarily, next to the forgotten jock strap or an open can of stale tennis balls. We sing our praises of sentences to the hanging clothes and walls. We parade around our images and imagine ourselves pulchritudinous women on streets, short skirted, daring to flash legs. We tell our jokes and believe we hear pales of laughter but it could be the curious nibblings of mice. So dark, here in the box of the prose poem. No wonder we lose our way. No wonder we grow angry or crazy. No wonder we resort to prestidigitations of words. We yearn for the shouting flight of lines that obtain high propagandistic altitudes; we crave the quaint oddities of verse punctuation. It is no wonder we like to paint the walls of the box with bitter tongues of irony. One day a child may go exploring in the closet. The child may open us up and her eyes could glow with illuminated pleasure. That's the picture we hold in our imaginations. We push away the one with the toy poodle in it—he who sniffs around, noses open our home, and chews our paragraphs to pieces.

Puritan

It's clarity—not cleanliness—that pals with Godliness.
Go wash your hands and then when you come back
I'll explain:

A sentence performs best when it is clearly written
or when clearly spoken. People know what to do and
don't start acting like chickens with their heads cut
off running bloody into each other. Imagine signs that
read, "STOP, MAYBE" or "POSSIBLE RAILROAD
CROSSING."

Of course you want your water crystal clear, and you'll
dole out higher taxes to get rid of the smog over your
city and in your lungs. Another word for clarity you
like, holding a fine glass of Riesling up to the light,
is the longer word, transparency. We want to be able
to see what the fat cat politicians and the Wall Street
bankers are up to, and geneticists are working night
and day on DNA modifications to meet our future
needs. Soon our skin will be transparent like many
species of tropical fish. You will be able to peer inside
to determine if you've got a plugged artery or cirrhoses
of the liver. Health costs will plummet with better self-
diagnosis.

Won't it be fun watching the turkey and cranberry
sauce go down on Thanksgiving? Magicians will
have an easier time reading minds. The divorce rate
will plummet because you will be able to see your
significant other's true or untrue heart. Once we get
the earth beneath us transparent it will be easier to

eliminate moles and possums from our yards, and we'll know better when volcanoes are about to blow. Think of the time and lives saved. No wonder people fondle their diamond rings. One quick look and they know how clear the world could be. They know that clarity is no utopian ideal but probably possible.

Have we locked them up? Have we caught them all, anyone left who still smokes and still prefers the opaque and impure? I hear they've taken all the l-a-n-g-u-a-g-e poets to Guantánamo Bay.

Query

My old empire, it's debt ridden and its infrastructure pipes are plugged up. If you held an auction at the storage unit, would anyone come, take and look and make a bid? I have a queasy feeling it's been going through a long season of bad hair days—more than dry hair or split ends or hair falling out or graying. I'd say the problem's been going on more than a decade and Rogaine won't do much good.

When empires grow old, do they wear their trousers rolled? I'm afraid buying more expensive conditioner works only in the morning if you stay inside and out of the sun. Plastic surgery, hair or breast implants, drones, just don't do the job for this or any old empire.

Have you taken a quiet stroll lately through the graveyard of empires, next to the Wasteland Disposal Plant, out behind the animal shelter? Arnold Toynbee (1889-1975) is buried there along with his twelve volumes, sealed in watertight plastic, on the rise and fall of civilizations. The place has lots of other archeological ruins, most of which are blank, half buried beneath the march of fallen leaves.

Question

Suppose Fiction set out like a schoolmarm with a ruler to teach us how to separate love from sex?

Look at Elizabeth Taylor, Fiction says. She never had sex before marriage. Look where it got her. She likes to hang around gay men and couldn't hang on to her young stud of a construction worker husband. What a shame with all that money and all those perfumes!

You separate love from sex the same way you remove the words written from the paper, Fiction says. You say the words out loud, or you type them from the paper into your word processor.

You separate love from sex the same way you get fleas out of a carpet. Of course tears are part of the process. You separate love from sex the same way the inside stays inside and the outside stays outside at home. You use chemical foggers. Set one of those suckers down on a newspaper in every room and in your attic, push the button down and then leave the house for twenty-four hours.

You separate love from sex, Fiction says, the same way that, with a razor blade, you peel off your skin.

Reader as Ann Landers

Richard Brautigan did not begin as a writer. He began as a salesman of used streams and waterfalls out of a huge warehouse on the border in El Paso. In those days the neo-capitalists of Mexico City were buying up the old haciendas and those haciendas needed more than the dust swept out of them. They needed sprucing up with spruces, streams streaming, and waterfalls falling. If Richard had stuck to selling off movable appliances from nature he would have had a steady income and avoided the financial ups and downs of writer's royalties and never fallen for the fable that no books means no money means no pussy. Richard my friend, the writing business is no business. I wish you'd taken my advice. What fun we could have had together, if you'd made it to old age, tinkering with some mechanical cosmos we'd manufactured down in our basement.

Remembering Freud

Regan hasn't gotten over the idea we'd be happier if we rolled around in bed and had sex all the time. Now here's a utopia we've reached briefly in our lives at least a couple of times. It may have lasted a weekend. It may have lasted two weeks or maybe three months. The thing is, we had it, most of us, and therefore Regan expresses understanding and sympathy for the promiscuous and the sex addicts, those who have ridden to the top of the mountain, to an actual utopia, and seek it out again and again, over and over, in the dim bars of their drinks.

Is it love, this utopia of sheets? No it's not, but it was the first step on the road to love.

New pathways were cut by light through the dark cavities of brains. Unidentified rain forest orchids bloomed gracefully all over flesh. They know what they're seeking and wish to regain what actually existed, unlike dreamer utopian socialists, anarchists, and free market capitalists. They know, like the advertisers know and the ideologues never guess, that it's sex, not money, that sells and remains at the heart of the American dream, the rapid running, the pursuit of happiness.

Restless as a Windshield Wiper Blade

Being a male is an art in the South, an art Rene is trying to learn as a man from New York City who graduated from an Arts Magnet High School majoring in religious music. Rene works playing the great organ in the main downtown Atlanta Catholic church, but Rene knows he got low marks at a neighborhood block party when he couldn't discuss football.

Tough as a hickory rail.

Both the gents and ladies started making slightly hostile humorous remarks when Rene said he was a vegetarian and never had tried barbeque. Go ahead, they said, it won't kill you. Then a guy asked Rene if he wanted a shot of Wild Turkey and he said he didn't know there were any turkeys left in the wild to shoot. The guy didn't appreciate the humorous remark.

Tough as lawnmower tires.

Rene's got a four-year old daughter and one August afternoon Rene took Rachel and her friend Rosten hiking in the woods out at Cherry Creek Park. It got so sweaty Rene took off his shirt. The girls asked if they could remove their shirts and Rene said sure. When Rene took home Rachel's friend Rosten, who has a charming extra sixth toe on her left foot—well, her mother got a bit furious for exposing her daughter's imaginary breasts to the trees.

Tough as a boiled mother-in-law.

A couple of years later Rene was helping take care of a six-year-old girl whose parents were divorced. The father was a soldier stationed in El Paso at Fort Hood, recently returned from Iraq, going through post-traumatic stress disorder. The mother, another soldier, had been sent to Afghanistan to look under women's burkas for weapons or bombs. Just for fun, after Darleen got done sharpening every pencil they had in the house, Rene painted Darleen's fingers and toes with his daughter's red nail polish.

Men don't put nail polish on girls, the grandma said.

What could Rene say? I'm a Yankee from New York City, where life tips a bit toward the avant-garde.

Tough as hog's breath.

San Antonio Fish Man

I had an old friend named Sanders. I'd known him twenty years, and he had such an odd way of talking I wish now I'd taped him. Sanders didn't have a regular home. He lived in a U-Lock-'Em storage unit about a mile from his mother's house. I'd start to talk to Sanders about the problems I was having with my son skipping school, and then he would reply by talking about massive plankton die-off caused by ocean pollution that would lead to lack of oxygen and to all of us suffocating to death. I'd tell Sanders about how I couldn't get my wife to come into Dallas. All she'd do is stay in our old house out in East Texas, even though she hated the small town more than the city. I tried to get her to come on the weekends, so we could go hear live music or see an art film in the evenings, but Sanders would start jawing about a creek not far from the place where I worked where we'd be bound to find ancient Indian arrowheads and even shards of pottery.

One day it was me and Sanders and Salado hanging out in the bookstore. Salado and I are writers and we like talking writer stuff—I can't remember exactly what we were discussing—and Sanders kept butting in wanting to talk about his brother over in Austin opening a pottery shop, so I finally said to Sanders, "Look, when you want to change the subject, announce it. Say something like, 'Do you mind if I change the subject?' That way people won't get irritated and feel like punching you out." That didn't work, so Salado got a piece of paper and wrote in great big letters on the paper what we were talking about—something

123

like "POETRY AND ACTIVISM" — and he held it out from his chest so that Sanders could see it at all times. "I LIKE YOU, SANDERS. I REALLY DO," Salado kept saying. Then Sanders started talking about the San Antonio fish man who was draining the aquifer. Salado took the piece of paper with our subject on it and waved it up and down in front of Sander's face. I shouted, "THIS IS WHAT WE'RE TALKING ABOUT, THIS IS WHAT WE'RE TALKING ABOUT!" Sanders said "I'm trying. I really am," but we went out the door of the store and got in Salado's car and drove off leaving Sanders to run the store by himself. For years we'd put up with him and we couldn't stand it any longer. Finally, after about fifteen minutes, as we were pulling up to a bar, I said to Salado, "Maybe he wants us to write poems about the San Antonio fish man and have a demonstration out there."

Saɳdy

My buddies had always told me never to mention any details about sex when dating a woman. That it not only killed the romance but killed the relationship. I ran a study on two ladies I was dating, wanting to believe that honesty was possible in a relationship, but sure enough, a single comment, like "I bet you have great nipples. I hope to put honey on them and have a suck some day," killed things instantly.

So imagine my surprise when a woman I'd been dating every night for a week suddenly said, as I helped her on with her coat at the front of her apartment, "Let's check into a fancy motel after we finish the Chinese and fuck each other's brains out."

I was stunned. "Maybe I'll do more beer than food," I stuttered out, trying to be witty. "I'm just kidding," I added.

We ate out Chinese on Congress Street in Austin, and then walked down to the Colorado to check into one of the bigger hotels. Sandy was twelve years younger than I. I chalked her directness up to a change in women that I was unaware of. I anticipated that this would be a good change once we got in bed. She would tell me what to do to please her—hopefully not like a drill sergeant—and I would do it. What could be better? No more guessing.

We asked for a room that was non-smoking and had a good view of the river. When we got to the room, however, we could both smell cigarettes.

"I can't do it in a room that stinks of nicotine," Sandy said.

"Well, we could do it in the shower. The water and the soap perfumes should get rid of the smell."

"No, no," said Sandy. "We'll go downstairs and get another room."

"How about back at my place — or yours?"

"No, we need something special to mark this special night."

"I'm terribly sorry, the man at check-in explained, "but there's a convention going on and it's the only room available. It was a nonsmoking room but I guess the last guest broke the rules."

"I forgot to check," I said. "Does the room have a balcony?"

"All the rooms on the river side have balconies."

"What are you suggesting?" Sandy said. "That we move the bed out and sleep on the balcony?"

"It could be a ... special adventure."

"No thanks. I am afraid of heights. Get your money back."

"We could go out to Onion Creek State Park, fifteen minutes away. I've got a rubber mat and sleeping bags. We could sleep in the back of my pickup, look out at the moon. It'll be too dark to put up my pup tent."

"Sir, sir, after you give him his money back, could you call me a cab?"

Scholar

Scot is not a scholar or critic of masterful texts. He has a new field, a field never before investigated. Scot is the scholar of letters slipped inside forgotten books. He haunts old bookstores flipping through texts. There is, of course, the letter Eugene O'Neill wrote to his lover, Louise Bryant, who was married to the man who wrote *Ten Days that Shook the World* and is buried in the Kremlin wall.

John Reed, her husband, found that letter in the poems of Whitman. If he had not found that letter and been disturbed enough to leave he might not have witnessed the Bolshevik take over of the Russian revolution.

Books given by those who have found themselves rescued by a book — often these are people who don't read many books — yet their letters are just as sacred. Scot found one from a single woman to a married man. He had told her he had nothing to offer, and she tried to explain how she didn't want anything. She wanted to see him. She was curious, she said, about married life.

From his scholarly researches on letters and notes folded inside books Scot widened his interests to include both marginal notes and inscriptions in the book by one person and given in the book to another. Most famous perhaps are the marginal notes of Samuel Taylor Coleridge and Herman Melville. Inscriptions usually appear on the recto of the front flyleaf or on the front of the title page.

These inscriptions, which he finds in used bookstores all over the country, fill him—a solitary man—with a melancholy concerning the human prospect. There are conventions somehow learned and followed by these writers, so it is possible to present here the essential Urtext:

The inscriber says in many ways, either direct or indirect, that he or she loves the inscribee. The inscriber explains that the words in the book are his or her most intimate thoughts that he or she is not able to put into words himself or herself. The inscriber indicates that by giving the inscribee the book he or she is giving a whole or part of who he or she is to the inscribee. In essence, the book is the ritual gift of the soul.

Scot's melancholy comes from the fact that anyone once so loved could sell such a ritual gift, such a revealing of another's heart, to a clerk in a strange store for the cold transaction of cash. Yet it happens all the time. Scot's collection contains over a thousand such inscribed books, a true testament to the power of words in people's lives.

Scholars must attempt to understand. Suppose the love affair or a Platonic friendship ended badly. Suppose he or she is married to someone else. The inscribee may be afraid the new love will get jealous if he or she finds evidence of the old love around. Not only books have this power. Scot has known women who have married divorced men only on condition that the men sell the houses they loved and fought to keep in the divorce settlements from the former spouses. As far as friendship goes, seeing a book on the shelf with an inscription from a former friend or lover could cause painful sense of time passing and mortality. Finally you decide to sell the book.

But we must remember that the book is a relatively small object. A precious inscribed book might be tucked away somewhere in a closet, or kept hidden under the seat in a car, to be pulled out and enjoyed perhaps every few years at a traffic light. We don't pull out our fingernails. We don't cut off our fingers.

Ah, but Scot is a solitary scholar, a bachelor. Perhaps, after decades, inscriptions by an inscriber seem empty or hypocritical. There may be also, deeply hidden in the words, anger or pain or anxiousness about a loss soon anticipated. The gift of the inscribed book, in many cases, may be a last ditch attempt to hang on.

More research is needed. Always, of course, more research.

Shake It

Hey you over there, salt of the earth. Yeah you. Are you worth your salt? Shane is talking to you. Please don't take it with a grain of salt, it's time you reached across the tablecloth, if you're worth your salt, it's time you set down your silver fork and knife, it's time you wiped your face with your swank napkin, time you put down your crystal water glass and quit talking to the socially connected around you. Don't take what Shane has to say with a grain of salt. Whatever you're doing down there, Shane doesn't want this to be, for you, an "off-to-the-salt-mines" situation. Yeah, it's you Shane is addressing, you with the crooked and bright blue bow tie. Now's the time for you to pass the salt down to the end of this table for others to use — the salt that contains rainforests and seas and mud and winds and stars. It was made by millions of years and contains trace elements necessary for human life. If there's anything we all can't stand at the human table, that puts many of us in a sad mood, it's the hogs out there in the world wanting everything for themselves without giving one grain. Gandhi marched his followers to the sea and saw them beat bloody for the right to salt, to be merely, like you, salt of the earth.

Techniques for Revising Above the Real

#1. When you first write, make sure that each sentence is a good sentence, but also make sure that each sentence has no relation to the sentence that comes before or after it. For assistance, consult your nearest clown.

Example: See Spot run. Men and wine are fun. Cows take turns babysitting.

#2. When you revise what you have written, make two new sentences that use the words, and only the words, of your previous sentences. For assistance, consult a child before speech has been acquired.

Example: See Spot run, take turns babysitting. Cows, men, and wine are fun.

#3. When you make your final revision, keep in mind that the symbols used for the written word, and the sounds generated from the written word, are purely arbitrary. No archeological evidence exists for the Tower of Babel, for the corruption of some humanly spoken, divinely given tongue. For assistance, go to Catholic confession. You should hear whispered to you, "Technique's all a matter of magic."

Example: Sitting baby cows Spot. See, men run and are fun. Take turns, wine.

The Trouble with Nature

is that it's all too green. So let's thank the blue god of sky, thank the spring god for the little flower dots of color, thank the winter god for taking the green away with snow. How'd you like it if all the houses and buildings were green like the lawns of suburbia? One grand omnivorous salad, Nightmare! Then nature comes along with white fungi, the atom bomb shaped mushrooms my daughter has refused to eat since she was four. Nature needs a good public relations firm. She needs more than Smokey the Bear and the Jolly Green Giant. What if you woke up one morning and found little green men had come in and painted your skin, your teeth, your hair—all the color of money, green? It happened to a friend of mine in a dank basement apartment near the San Antonio Trinity River. He looked in the mirror to shave and found his mouth full of bright green moss. I'd tell you my friend's name but you might know him. No wonder people hide in air-conditioned cars and houses, and have no concern for the environment or global warming. Things will only improve when we can deposit leaves as cash.

The Unsung

Behind my three-story brick house, in the apartment above the stone garage—behind my house on Mesa in the barely American city of El Paso—lived, back in 1986, the Panamanian dictator Noriega's former masseuse.

In my brick house in 1972, over in the back of the tall attic where I built a false wall, lived Greg, the marijuana dealer who believed he could start a revolution in consciousness by going from door to door turning everyone on. He later smuggled guns from Mexico to the Weathermen in the Rockies.

Behind this built-in shelf of books, which opens up to reveal a hidden room, my great-great-grandfather, who built this Sunset Heights home, hid slaves from east Texas plantations, surprisingly smuggled to El Paso, a village then, when everyone believed the Underground Railroad went only north to Canada. They slipped over the border into Mexico around the mountain then west of town, where today, perched on top, sits the great concrete statue Cristo Rey.

Truth

"What is truth?" the twenty-third clown asked, rolling out of the midget car in the circus ring. Everyone clapped. The circus band began to play. The tubas and trombones counterpointed each other asking, *What is truth? What is truth!*

The twenty-third clown was a famous, sad clown. No one was frightened by his sad-dark-teary-face because his depressing look made him seem a tad pitiful and weak. People laughed and felt superior.

The clown stood in the spotlight with his white hat and black pants and swept the truth around in the spotlight with a broom. Gradually the spotlight dimmed and shrank and then truth — what was left of it — the light, it got swept under the rug. The clown picked up the rug and shook the dust off, but the truth, it had vanished.

Understanding Needed

A recent study has confirmed that guns have mineral consciousness, and although paralyzed from birth and incapable of self-movement, they seem aware that they have been used to kill many life forms, including humans.

Communicating telepathically with renowned author, shoemaker, and psychic Chuck Taylor through the soles of his feet, the whole gun and weapon's community wishes to inform humans that it suffers utterly from horrendous guilt over the deaths of millions upon millions since firearms first were invented and aimed at innocent living beings, as if the firearms were blood-hungry pointer canines.

Gun support groups and gun therapists have met with whole armories of weapons—despite the protests of the NRA—to assist these victimized firearms in the grieving and healing process, to stop the tears and the rusting. We need to honor and support these noble weapons that have gone bravely to battle and done their duty, loyally following the commands of the hands that held them.

Of course a small minority of guns exist that have refused to fire or have misfired, as well as an even smaller minority of true believers ready to return to the slaughter at any moment, under any circumstances, but the vast majority of weapons would be happy to remain on display in their cases, safely locked up and away from children, monuments like Auschwitz to

136

barbarous times, yet occasionally taken out to enjoy a cleaning caress of a hand holding an oil cloth.

Understanding the Amazon

What man worth his salt has not spent part of his life searching for the Amazon? Anyone who saw the poster of Raquel Welch in *One Million Years BC* knows what Urban means.

Where are you O where are you when Urban needs you, Amazon? Humans have traveled up some mighty rivers. Humans have walked the docks and shorelines of Turkey and many a Greek island.

It's not that we're looking for someone to fight our wars, it's not that we're sick of wandering the woods and hills trying to kill lions and bears, meat for the family, we wish to meet a woman, you know, that can meet us eye to eye, no looking down, a women who doesn't feel crushed if we're on top, a woman who likes the smell of axle grease as much as the smell of baby poop, and doesn't mind getting under a vehicle to fix the brakes.

A less binary world is what Urban is getting at. Sparks still are going to fly, mind you, but imagine for a moment the peace that would come from turning down the volume of dualism, whose cacophony for millennia has harried Western life.

Unexamined Life

Ursula, for the first time in half a decade, finds herself around people who are content talking about whatever passes through their minds. She is a classical scholar, a student of Sappho and Aristophanes, and here she is with a woman who is commenting on a blouse she tried on and almost bought a Dillard's, a silk thing with a tropical pattern—and then the man with the woman says he didn't like the Batman movie *The Dark Knight* and his car almost got hit coming out of the parking lot when it started to rain. Ursula is older now and more patient. She considers how her life might have been if she had *not* decided, back in high school, that the characters in Shakespeare's play, *The Merchant of Venice*, were more fascinating than her fellow classmates. Why in the world did she find religious bigotry so interesting? Because the boy she loved then was a Jew, and got beat up on the school bus. Things like that happen all the time. Later Ursula lets the young couple ramble on at their table at Starbucks, and imagines the shadows of clouds in the puddles of her cracked driveway. What if she had taken the road more commonly traveled? Well, she has six grandchildren, and has been married forty-four years, in succession, to three different men. Only a large amount of unexamination could have accomplished these feats.

Unlyric Essay

Pair of shoes, a woman's pair of black loafers, sitting on the tile and cement stairs, sitting on the tile and cement stairs about five steps up from the bottom, a pair of women's shoes on the stairs that lead up to the University side entrance to the Blocker Building. A pair of shoes present and an accounted for over a week, standing there, neatly tucked together, neatly parallel to each other. A proper pair of shoes. A quiet pair of shoes. When the woman took off her shoes and left them so properly did she leave her proper life behind? A man, let's say, with a beard and long hair pulled up on a Harley. The man is a famous medieval scholar and just finished giving a lecture on the troubadour poets. The great scholar does not believe in married love. He tells the women in the prim loafers she is a princess and that she will never find a husband—they are all off, the good ones, fighting wars in the holy lands of oil, and she should get on his motorcycle and go with him to Mexico. "Leave the shoes behind," he says. "Your feet will be able to better grip the fold down bars on the back of my Harley Davidson without those prissy shoes. We'll be mostly walking the beaches of Mexico anyway, writing love lyrics in the sand. You do know Latin, don't you?"

Una asks, why are those shoes there, and how come the woman did not come back and get her shoes?

Una's seen those bicycles on campus, all covered in the calcium white of bird poop. This one's been locked to the same pole for the two years she's been walking behind the Blocker Building going to Evan's Library to work in a tiny carrel on her dissertation. What happened to the guy who owned the maroon English style bicycle? Did he die in a car accident? Did he drop out of school? Did a woman pull up on a black Harley and whisper, "Hey, handsome, want to blow this joint and go to Mexico?" Maybe the woman who left the shoes behind also left the bicycle behind? These shoes, that bicycle, they're driving Una loopy. She can't take the ambiguity. She can't take the not knowing. She can't take all the bird droppings. They should be scraped off and recycled into chalk for the university's blackboards.

Should Una come back tonight with a hacksaw and cut the bicycle free? The bike wants a bath, she's sure of it. The bike wants to feel again the wind around its handlebars. It wants to slide over the miles like an Olympic ice skater. Una loaned her bike to an extremely poor and soulful Russian fellow graduate student, the bicycle got stolen out of his backyard, and the poor graduate student never replaced her bike, so she is due this one.

Una takes the shoes home in her backpack. She covers them with gesso and puts them up on the family altar on the fireplace mantel. "This is the tomb of the unknown shoes," she tells her husband. That night Una drives up to campus around ten and parks her pickup next to the Blocker Building. She cuts free the bike with powerful clippers, lifts it quickly into the back of the pickup, and drives off. She feels half a criminal, half a hero. She's deprived the university of a few dollars from selling the bike at auction, but she's doing her part to solve (or at least settle) an unresolved mystery of the world. Her garage will now be — in the corner by the freezer where her husband stores the deer meat — after a proper scrubbing, the home of the unknown bicycle.

Maybe when her daughter Umbra gets older, she will learn to ride a bicycle, give it a name, and a resurrection will happen.

Vantage of Innocence

My father Vance said the wind could blow so hard that straw from the fields would stick in the telephone poles like long needles. We were close to the North Carolina coast and he parked in front of an old two-story hotel in an old town. "The eye of the storm is supposed to pass over here," he said to my sister Val. "What's a storm eye?" I asked, but my father did not answer.

We got a room on the second floor. My father told me to stand to the side of the window, not directly in front of it, and tell him if I began to see things blowing by. "I see branches, lots of branches, some of them big," I said.

Then the hotel caught on fire and we had to run outside in whatever we had on to stand in the wind and rain on the asphalt parking lot across the road waiting for the fire truck to show up. The fire truck arrived, unrolled its hoses, and put out the small fire around an electrical transformer close to the room we were staying in.

"I guess you can all go back in," the fire chief explained. "You've got to be kidding," my father answered. "We've got no place else to put you," the hotel man said quietly. Everyone was cold and soaking wet, glad to get out of the wind and back inside the hotel to dry off and change. My father spent a night in a chair back from the window, watching the wind outside and watching the transformer.

The year was 1954 and I was in the fourth grade. I

wasn't scared at all. I saw hurricanes as the way life should be every now and then—as great adventure, as a chance, kindly provided by the universe, for masculine heroism.

The next morning we three got back in the old Buick and drove on to Chapel Hill. The roads were wet all the way but there was no standing water. Things were, once again, in the vantage of the normal.

Virgin Manifesto

Vito tried to present his view during lunch with friends at the Whole Foods on Greenville in Dallas, and all he got was laughed at. One friend pointed at the white hairs in his beard and told him he was way behind the times.

Vito doesn't have to listen to laughter if he presents his ideas here at the table of fiction. Twenty years have passed since he opened his mouth, although the laughter still rings in his ears.

He'll start with an axiom. Virginity is a position of power. Elizabeth the First, Queen of England (1533-1603), was the Virgin Queen. When a woman opens her legs however, when she opens that door and lets the stranger in to drop his seed, she has, unless it is rape, voluntarily ceded her virginity and no longer possesses the absolute power over her body that she possessed in a state of virginity.

Why has she voluntarily ceded absolute power to be seeded? Well, Vito is a man here, and can only guess. She has, perhaps, ceded autonomy because of the physical pleasure involved, the letting go. No one wants to be absolutely sovereign like a lonely Queen who at a whim can have people beheaded. No one wants that separation. A woman seeks love, seeks union, a sharing, a conversation, an intimacy — that is impossible for a Virgin Queen in a lonely tower. Like Rapunzel, most women choose to let down their golden hair, and is it not always golden, one way or another, to the lover?

The man has ceded his virginity too. That is what the sexual exchange does. A joining happens and both parties are no longer independently sovereign. Joining has happened, a kind of wedding has happened, in the act of making love, and there's the possibility that the journey has begun for a third person with the fertilizing of the egg by the sperm—or is it the fertilizing of the sperm by the egg?

If the journey has begun then the two makers of the child stand together in a trust to tend to the security, health, and rights of this new being. They are parents to this new being together and neither parent has total autocratic sovereignty. That was lost in the act of love. Those who want total authority over their bodies need to remain virgins.

Therefore the feminist argument that says this is my body and I get to decide all by myself whether the living being in my uterus lives or dies is a false argument. Such absolute sovereignty ends in the act of sex when two people join, when a woman opens her legs and lets another in. It is a grave moral error for a woman to have an abortion without consulting her partner. It is a grave moral error if a man agrees to take the child and raise the child and signs a legally binding document to do so, yet the woman dictatorially proceeds with an abortion.

She is no longer a Virgin Queen, an absolute source of power. For every feminism let there be a masculism. Sisters and brothers, for every testament to women's rights, let there be a testament to men's rights.

War

I'm sorry, man, I'm sorry for you and your ex, getting sent over to the war, the two of you. Even though they got Saddam, they never found weapons of mass destruction.

Like, I've got this small house. I mean, I'd like to do the patriotic thing but I've got three cats and a dog and a wife in this tiny one bedroom. I know I'm your oldest friend. We go way back. The crazy things we used to do in high school, selling a little pot to friends, you know, and borrowing cars. Maybe we should have spent less time skipping classes and driving around and I wouldn't be working at Wally Mart and you'd have gotten that football scholarship to UTEP and wouldn't of had to enlist.

We could be college grads, making good money with homes in the Coronado neighborhood, but we did what we did, didn't we guy, and things came down as they did, and so here we are, running into each other here at Hooters like old times, and now you're a papa. That is so cool.

I dig your courage and your drive to protect our freedoms, what with nine-eleven, but hey, what about an uncle or something? I know you never knew your mom or your dad and grew up in an orphanage, but everybody's got family out there somewhere and this is their time to step up and do their part for those who're making the sacrifice.

You know my mom had breast cancer and passed? It was hard cause it happened so fast and I'm strapped, still paying for her funeral. We're both lucky though. You remember Warley who played center our senior year? He went to Afghanistan and when he came back he found out his wife got pregnant by another man. He could count the months in his head but he held out for the DNA test. He wasn't the same after that. He volunteered for Iraq and got blown up a mile from the green zone while giving candy to kid. The kid was killed too, suicide bomber I heard.

I think about Warley when I'm stocking the shelves in automotive. I start crying, but you know I can't get mad at his old lady—you must have been in a class or two with Wendy, pretty and flirty—she was never the kind to be by herself, she'd had boyfriends going back to first grade. Boy she had a rack on her better than a lot of these gals. Catch a look at that blonde by the restroom. Lord a' mighty, sets the blood to boil. Guess we've got some of the old jet fuel left in us.

I bet you're a great dad, I bet you got your boy in helmets and pads even though he's barely out of kindergarten, I bet Wanda is the super-mom, Wanda always wanted to be a mom, you could tell that back in elementary school, always drawing those crayon pictures of big smiling families, and I remember being your best man in the wedding chapel downtown in El Paso. You didn't want nobody to find out cause you were both still in school and living separate, she with her family and you at the orphanage, and then you guys dropped out of school and got that little house over on Grand. I was still with Whitney and we'd come over and barbeque and toss the pigskin around in the street and you helped me change the brake pads on the orange Toyota.

You'd think once the grandkid came along her parents would have mellowed, forgiven her running off with you, and the drug and alcohol shit we all did for the glory of it. You got cleaned up and straightened out and we got back to going to church. You both joined the service and both got sent to Fort Hood I heard. I guess you got busy and couldn't write or send emails.

Too bad it didn't work out with Wanda in the end. What's the divorce rate these days? Fifty percent? I'm not going to pry and ask what happened. I got enough friends divorced and they're still trying to figure out what happened. Wanda liked to drink. But who doesn't? Didn't she burn down this friend's house over Christmas vacation? Word got around she got kicked out of the army for collecting dependent money for the kid when he'd been staying at the friend's house that later burned down, but you never know whether to believe what you hear on the street.

I'm sorry man. It's great you got back home here to El Paso, before they ship you out to Iraq. I can't believe they can send you both at the same time. They know you're the parents, right? It must be some military paper pusher's mistake. We work these odd shifts, Wendy and I, rotating from days to nights to days since the Wal-Mart went twenty-four hour. We hardly sleep together or ever see each other. That's our life, man. We're exhausted all the time and all I got is the same beat up orange Toyota.

I'm sorry. You know I never liked kids. I never had any brothers or sisters. I'm sorry, man—you want another beer? I'm sorry …

War Dream

Like the flashing of swords the rumor passed through the troops and the armies stopped fighting.

The knights led the way, turning their horses away from the field where the blood ran like rivers, galloping into the pine woods surrounding like a vast army holding pikes. Foot soldiers dropped their swords and shields. All streamed away toward their own realms.

Those in charge did not parlay or speak to each other for fear of spies who might assist the enemy. When I reached my own estate after two days riding, I found the castle deserted. Bodies lay strewn in nearby fields. No sign of life—except for the old woman who grew herbs and lived in an oak grove a half-day's ride from my lands.

I tortured the old woman. She screamed that the gods had forbidden her to speak. A plague had come, she finally confessed, and all had been taken—my dogs, my servants, my field hands, my wife and my two children. In two days, shedding tears, I buried my wife and children and those of the household of royal blood and said the chants of the ancestors over the graves.

"What man has done this?" I asked the old woman before I killed her. She said he rested now in a cave in the high mountains. He wanted nothing more to do with his kind and spoke only of the gods.

I hurried on. To reach the mountains I had to skirt the

shore of a barren salt lake. A score of peasants tried to stop me. I broad axed a few, but my horse quickly outran the others.

All day through deep woods I traveled hearing voices cursing my line. Someone threw rocks from the top of a ravine. When I reached the foothills the winds were behind me. I fell to my knees in an opening in the thickets and prayed to the rock god of the mountains for a blessing.

Later I abandoned my mount and crawled on my belly eating berries wherever I found them in the thorny brush. On high ground, above the tree line, I surprised a lynx with two babies and crushed their skulls with a rock and my fists. I feasted on an open fire, regaining my strength, chewing the gut into strings and drying the skins to make clothing. Then I followed the invisible trails higher.

The thin air made me dizzy. At times I lost my step and slid back and nearly plunged into the ravines on either side of the rise I followed up and up into ice and snow. The wind no longer was behind me. It whipped my face sore and my beard grew icicles. I did not sleep for days. I climbed by day and by night by the light of the hard cold stars. Finally I reached the cave. Large bones lay at the entrance.

There was a circle of ashes and in the ashes were markings I could not read. I was weeping and could not cry out. I tore off the animal skin I wore as a shirt, tied it with the gut to a stick, and with my flint lit a torch. "Come out," I whispered as I entered the darkness. "I come to humbly serve, to always do your bidding. Did I not take up arms as you said? Speak, my Father."

Weaᵏ **Bladder**

"I opened my eyes when you came into the room," Wesley's mother said. "Why didn't you stay by the bed longer?"

"You weren't speaking. You weren't moving," Wesley replied. "I put my hand on your head. I told you I loved you. Although I know that love is more than a feeling, I was feeling, I was in pain."

"But you left the room. You should not have left my bedside. I was dead when you came back. You should have held my hand until I passed."

"Ma," Wesley said, "remember those long car drives when I was five and you and dad would never stop and I ended up going in my pants?"

Why I Love Prose Poems

Whittaker wrote that to get your attention. Whittaker doesn't hate or love prose poems, but narratives whose subjects are narratives—he doesn't worry about political correctness here—he's prejudiced, he disapproves of them before he reads them and after he reads them. Whittaker can smell such a narrative a block off, like the smell of dead fish on a beach. Actually, that's not it. Imagine a grease trap from a fried food restaurant emptied into an alley. The thing is, a narrative, whatever its kind, must not mean but be. It's palpable and mute, like bottled fruit. (Catch the plagiarism?)

Anyway, prose poems and mini-stories will lie around clogging the corners long after Whittaker and this world of readers are gone. Do you disapprove of rocks? Do you have a grudge against trees? Any disapproval— don't you see?—is impotent, a grain of sand quickly picked out of Mr. Limpkin's eye. Whittaker has been charmed by certain narratives, yes, he admits it, like the folktale about the father and the boy and the horse called "Justice," by Delmore Schwartz, but that was a long time ago. It's been years since their eyes met. But dislike prose poems and mini-stories, no. He'll leave that to others. Whittaker is not going to belittle himself that way. When approached by a narrative that doesn't do anything for him, he politely refuses to dance, and since he disapproves of narratives about narratives, let's see no more.

"The letter X is the twenty-fourth letter of the alphabet and is derived from the fifteenth letter in the Proto-Sinaitic alphabetic, samekh. In Hebrew, samekh means "support, the act of supporting."

—Ouaknin, *Mysteries of the Alphabet*

There is no commentary on Y and Z.

Xerox This, Friend

In the bland of our daily jobs, Rob and I, let us take
note of Xenia, from over the fence, who never cuts the
backyard grass and has let the trees come back, of Xenia
who keeps a swayback pig, who brings us Christmas
presents every year, sipping nutmeg in our kitchen
nook, complaining of her three-day stress of surgeon's
work; ah Xenia, from over the fence, who calls her ex-
husband out in California twice a week (though he is
married wealthier to a computer exec), yes Xenia from
over the fence, sons in Austin who are bankers and
never call, Xenia, who when we are eating together at a
restaurant, lets her eyes follow the women walking as
well as the men; Xenia, hair thinning and overweight,
ex-farm girl 4-H barrel rider from Coleman County
Texas; from over the fence, Xenia handing me a Shiner
from her leather cooler, or conversely doing eighty at
three a.m. down interstate 35 in her silver Mercedes,
raising always the noble and mortal questions when
we talk — *Why the hell are we here, and what's the meaning
of all this?* Xenia, note, as you are swerving lane to lane
onto the shoulders of the road, the meaning is, the
meaning is, JUST IS, and Xenia, my husband Rob and
I, we're so glad you're here. We don't know why. We
can't explain, but you give us meaning. You support.

Xylophone of Love

Can a poem be a love poem if it declares itself to be a
love poem, or must the poem have gallons of love in its
heart? What if my longest love has been books? I am a
polygamist of books, a man so long in love with shelves
of dusty pages. I have, for a moment, fallen deeply for
the ladybug landing on my sleeve, and over the years
many ladybugs have come and never done a drop of
harm. Can I honestly say that I love ladybugs, and that
they are true ladies? Am I in love with their orange
coloration? Am I in love with the black dots? I *am* in
love with the moment's hesitation that exists between
the unfolding of their wings and their taking off? Can
I say in a love poem that I am scared of love? Can I
say that I've never loved an elephant though the tired
folds beneath their eyes entrance me always? Can I tell
you that I am in love with lowing sounds of distance
through the morning mist? Can I tell you I love the
sound water makes when you move your legs slowly
wading up a running stream? Can I tell you I love the
way two dogs will touch their lips of noses together,
that I'm in love with the circular wrinkles made on
the skin of lakes by the water strider? Who cannot be
in love with rocks, so reliable and silent? I have yet
to have an argument with a rock. I will tell you I love
watching squirrels chase each other in the tall elms of
Elmhurst, my hometown. These magnificent aerialists
spell love and death leaping around on branches green
in their ferocious bodies. I cannot love a game that is
not done for the fun of it. I have no love for games that
require tickets or spectators. Can I say I loved playing
football with no equipment on summer vacant lots,

even though I nearly got my front teeth knocked out? Do I still love my first girlfriend from kindergarten who had long black beautiful hair? We would hide from the teachers, holding hands through playtime behind a small green shed set in the corner of the playground. Her name was Geraldine. I fell in love with a man once, in Salt Lake City in 1979, buying a special light for a slide projector in a light bulb store. Love at first sight it was and I wanted to live with him forever. Love is never pure. It is full of self-interest. Love can tie you down as it sets you free. Love can kill you with its stings of the immortal. But is our earthly love immortal? I say the jury's out but then my Mormon friends say families live in heaven together and family love is immortal. For a moment I am a Mormon, but then I'm not so sure I want to spend immortal time with my father or mother, though I love them for the gift of life and for their caring. I have no idea what love is. I play the xylophone of love in my ribs. Is there a creature alive that knows? I didn't always love the five children I played a part in bringing up. How can anyone write a love poem when we only fumble around in the sheets of dark, occasionally making sparks? I think that Erich Fromm came closest when he said in *The Art of Loving* that love's a practice. We must practice, practice, practice, working out in the gym of love, and that's a lot of sweaty labor, and you may never get in shape. It's possible to love some people sometime but not all the people all the time. All you need is love, some famous rockers sang. We love the things we love for what they are, Frost the poet wrote.

Poet Frost wintered in San Antonio, and I've always loved the inner San Antonio, so I'm in love with the frosty locks of Robert Frost. That's the sense of love.

You may wonder why

conflicted people are more successful than people who know what they want. Take Yolana, for instance, she knew she wanted a rose tattoo on her butt. She got that rose tattoo on her butt, and a decade later she learned she got hepatitis C—I think it's C—or it could be A or D, I'm not sure. But Yoko, she kept wondering what her mother would think. "Your mother's not going to see your butt," I said, and she said, "Well, you've never seen our home and what do you know about the Chinese?" So Yoko debated and prevaricated and then they found out about the needles, you know, that they used to use to make tattoos.

Now me, I tend to have trouble with people who don't know what they want. You're in line behind one, and all you want is a cup of coffee with cream, and they can't decide on what it's going to be, a chocolate mocha with whipped crème on top, or the soup of the day. I want to shout babe, I don't mean to be mean, but you're already Rubenesque. I've never been conflicted, and I'm a failure. I'm not homeless yet, but I'm sixty and all I own is a green old Chevy van, and what I do is drive around outside of Austin up and down remote county roads looking for abandoned houses I can move into and pretend to rent. You may have seen me. I sell those bonsai plants in the parking lots of stores that have gone out of business. Stop by sometime and prevaricate. Take all the time you want to make up your mind. Come back tomorrow if you need to. Be like Shakespeare's Prince Hamlet. He dies at the end of the play, but it's only fiction, and the author had to figure out how to end things even though life goes on and on and is like the weather, always indecisive and changing. Buy or don't buy one of my bonsai. I've changed. I'm a better person now. More patient. Stay away from tattoos. I want you to live a long and happy life.

Youth

Yorath doesn't pass out wisdom. Not to nobody about nothing. He does his job and advice isn't part of the package or in his medicine bag of tricks. Why get yourself in trouble? Why break a heart?

But there the young man stood, a student from four years ago, missing half his teeth, his long hair a greasy tangle, working in the heat of August in the Mexican restaurant at the back of the Armadillo World Headquarters in Austin, Texas, where Willie Nelson and the Grateful Death often came to play. There he was, looking like one of the zombie dead, a speed freak or something, handing Yorath enchiladas through the service window, saying remember me, remember me? And this, a month after another student came up smiling in a coffee shop in her bare feet and told Yorath how exciting life was sleeping in a culvert up from Town Lake, living on the hippie streets of Austin.

"If it weren't for your class," the boy handing Yorath the food says, "if it weren't for reading that book, that Herman Hesse's *Steppenwolf*, things would not be so cool. I'd never have made it here."

"We come for the food," Yorath shrugs. "It's a place where my young boys can run around on the grass."

Zealous

The side shows! The side shows off the main circus tent! Do we have sideshows anymore, or only Sideshow Bob on *The Simpsons*? I suspect the real ones may be gone. It's turned politically incorrect, perhaps correctly so, to wonder at life's strange curves and bumps. We're told to boycott circuses. You have to settle with watching Disney's *Dumbo*, a much underrated animation masterpiece, or catch the long flight to Russia to view the Moscow Circus.

The circuses travelled by train from city to city all around our continental country. In the side show I saw a man take a five-foot-long sword — maybe you did too — and stick the point in a wooden tent pole so the blade stuck straight out with no assistance, all on its own. You knew that point was sharp.

I've seen the same sword cut through pineapples and coconuts to prove the blade's sharpness. Then I've watched the swallower of swords take up that sword. He stood on a small stage by himself. He had no chance to switch for a dull, phony sword with a retractable blade. I was the president of my high school magician's club. I knew all the moves.

I saw the circus man pick up all different sizes and types of blades from his table, and stick them down his throat, but when he pulled out the big sword stuck in the tent pole, that was the act's finale. He stood straight and raised his chin as high as he could and worked that gleaming blade into his mouth and down so slowly, so carefully, going for maximum dramatic effect.

What's the life expectancy of swallowers of swords? Can they carry major medical and life insurance?

Yes, I saw the blade go down and down, deep past the esophagus into the intestines, not to the hilt, but almost, maybe two inches short. I appreciated the training and bravery that went into the act. No doubt he began as a small child on his father's knee in a circus family, working with a butter knife at the breakfast table.

If you've seen the act you know it's fantastical and magical. You have stood in a pool of wonder. So many of the old circus acts fit the bill, like the man born with no arms who could remove a cigarette from a pack with his toes, stretch his right leg up and put the smoke to his lips, and then pull a Zippo lighter from the left pants' cuff, raise the lighter to the cigarette, and flip the level with a toe, lighting then his coffin nail. My grandfather Hall was with me when I saw the act in 1954, and he always called cigarettes coffin nails.

A little man there was who could stand on a metal plate almost boiling with electricity. He would jump on the plate, his hair would start standing up, and then his gorgeous assistant would hand him light bulbs that he could make glow brightly in his hands. He could hold a fluorescent tube between both hands and make it flicker and come alive.

I've read few books since technical school yet hunger to know, and am willing to pay, to be sure there exists the fantastical and magical. I won one time a whole case of circus Snickers Bars on a ten-foot-wide horizontal spinning wheel. I hid them away in my room, but then decided I was being silly and shared.

Was life a sword we needed to learn to swallow almost to the hilt?

Did you need to be a contortionist to survive?

I saw a man on a circus sideshow take a knife, feel carefully his upper arm for bone and vein, ligaments and nerve, and then slowly push the blade all the way through his arm. He had such discipline. He did it through the lower part of his leg also. I could see the muscle tremble slightly and terribly, but he talked to the audience all the time he was doing it, making humorous patter and little jokes. He never let out a cry and there was almost no bleeding. I have worked most of my life not to let out too many cries, to let out instead smiles and jokes.

Fantastic. Magical, the swords that come out of this life—but nothing has ever been as amazing as my grandma's homemade alphabetical soup.

Each bowl specialized on a single letter she cut from dough and cooked in the oven. The letters were larger and thicker than the canned soup kind. We'd eat the soup together around the table, Grandma, my sister and I, and we'd call out words that began with the soup letter of the day. *Amulet, amuck, amorous* on the day of the letter A. *Bamboozle, babushka, bazooka* on the day of the letter B. And so on through the fantastical, magical worlds of words and sounds. *Caboose! Doldrums! Euclidean! Fondue!* On and on.

Where did these circuses of words come from? They are high aerial acts dancing on our teeth and tongues, flipping over and out our mouths. Who invented them? When will corporations try to own them, and how did we ever get to know all these tricksters together over the infinite distances? Just look at the words we toss at one another's faces each day. How much care we have for one another! Sure, there comes at times a Hitlerian hate, but mostly it's love you know.

We are always, dear friends, zealous circus babies in our cribs, pulling at our toes, making the babbling *GOO, always haberdashery, ionosphere, jackanapes, kerfuffle, lickety-split* ... And it's no sideshow, it's the BIG TENT, the REALLY BIG SHOW, and most of the time we don't even know.

Zero Sum

may sound kind of glum, or ho hum, or dumb. Mr.
Nelson in ninth grade math would never have brought
into class the idea that you could add or sum things up
and end with zero. I added about five seconds between
the last period and the beginning of this sentence. I am
adding letters onto letters, adding empty space too, to
make up words that make up sentences. Are the spaces
zeroes if they mean something, if they carry a kind of
weight? Is the hole in the donut more than a hole if it
makes the dough into a donut, if it carries the power
of definition? If I eat around the hole and a space is
left do I still have the hole of a donut? Is Mr. Donut
still partially there even if I can't see him, or is this a
zero sum game? I could mount my camera on a tripod
and take a shot of the donut hole before and after the
donut being eaten. Of course new air will have blown
in and filled that empty space—few of the original
invisible nitrogen and oxygen atoms will still be
standing around. Suppose our bodies are the dough of
the donuts, and the hole is our soul. Without the hole
the body could not be defined as a body. It would be a
mere hunk of meat and not whole.

Because I am writing this prose poem in an email to
philosopher Michael, I find myself writing a kind of
philosophical comedy routine somewhat unlike what
I usually write. I can make this more poetic by saying
a few words like "a silver sliver of a moon in a dark
sky full of the sprinkles of whimsical stars." Stars and
moons always rev up a poem. Or I could talk about
"the tongue of the river lapping the dark and hungry

land." This one is a bit ominous. How about "the smile of the zebra hidden in the crouch of wildflowers?"

I am trying hard to avoid the subject of death. One could say life is a zero sum game. Experiences pile up upon experiences until the end, when you die, and then everything gets cancelled out. Yes, a zero sum game. That's death, or a mathematical view of death, and arguing with math is about as hard as arguing with the Catholic Church in the twelfth century. The soul could be the hole in the donut that makes us whole. It could be the organizing principle. You can have a bunch of car parts piled in your garage and have no car—no organizing principle, no intelligence operating, to put the car together so it runs correctly. You need the hole in the donut, the soul of the cosmos, to organize your elements into a round-wheeled running vehicle. God is the auto mechanic and baker of the universe. He can't be seen, like the hole in the donut.

Boy, writing a prose poem, with a philosopher on the line, at the other end of this email, sure is a zesty exercise. He probably won't read it all the way through. He'll throw up his hands in disgust at the faulty logic. Besides, everyone knows that you can't write philosophy except in French and German. No half-decent self-respecting philosopher will accept this proof of God based on an old joke heard by beginning philosophy majors sitting in the school cafeteria. Yes, there are female philosophy majors now, and they will tell you the donut hole is the vagina, and it is out that hole, that emptiness, life comes. It's never Sartre's *Being and Nothingness*. Rather it's nothingness and being. No mathematics is smart enough to sum down to death, or capable enough to ascend by subtraction up to God.

Zip-a-Dee-Doo-Dah, My Oh My What a Wonderful Day

It's time to get sensual. Right now Zimri's fingers are stroking a brick from his bookcase and it feels like sandpaper. If the rough spots were closer together and a bit stickier it would feel like a cat's tongue. He's constantly stroking his own body, to remind himself that he is still here. Zimri strokes his arms, one after another, up and down, driving to work clutching the steering wheel. A part he will stroke in public is his beard. He'll try to stop but will find his fingers weaving the beard hair again and again. He will look around an auditorium at other men to see how many others have their fingers in their beards close to their mouths. Zimri's had a few lovers ask to stroke his beard before they kissed the first time. They were curious, they wanted to know what they were getting themselves into. If it weren't for a lover Zimri never would have learned he had sharp teeth from chewing his nails as a kid. The beard chases away women Zimri never could be interested in anyway. He strokes his dog behind his ears and scratches his rump. The dog's hair is a little smoother than Zimri's beard but not as smooth as the hair on Zimri's head. Stroking others is often more rewarding than stroking oneself. Your fingers get the same sensation but you also get the happiness in other's eyes. Swimming, when he was an adolescent, would give Zimri erotic dreams that would wake him over and over at night, what with the body being stroked everywhere at once by gentle water hands. He likes stroking his legs. He likes rubbing oil on his feet that get dried out in the summer from wearing sandals. He likes rubbing on lip balm. When alone in bed Zimri takes pleasure in stroking his penis. What a silky smooth amazing thing you are, he thinks. Thank you for your softness and your tumescence, thank you for your excellent delivery system that has brought me countless hours of pleasure and three sensual children. What pleasure Zimri took in combing their hair as they sat on his lap. He could weep over the loss now they're too old and the pleasure has zipped away. Zimri's left lovers out of this fiction, out of respect for a shared privacy, but you know what lover's lips and tongues can feel and discover. Remember that old game where a friend walks up from behind and gently taps your head with a knuckle as if breaking an egg, and then strokes your hair in a downward movement with open palms to simulate the slow molasses slide of egg down your hair? It didn't fool Zimri. He can still smell the sensuous perfume of Zana when she stood close behind him and pulled that joke in his high school Latin class. A year ago Zimri got a gift from a recently divorced woman named Zoe in the process of rediscovering her sexuality. They were at a party, hundreds of people were around, but she gave Zimri a quick lovely kiss on the lips. That kiss was passed to her by the poet Robert Hass, who got it from the poet Allen Ginsberg, who got it from Sadakichi Hartmann, who got it from Walt Whitman. It was a chaste daisy chain kiss, yet still it tingles on his lips — not so much for its pedigree, but because it was a gift from Zoe, whom he still sees now and again at parties. She won't let him kiss her lips, but he does get to whisper "daisy chain" in her ear.

She smiles a cat smile.

Zimri's back home now, stroking again the rough bricks of his bookcase, but the thought of that kiss pulls him from his chair at times, and he will do a zany little shuffle dance about his tiny place.

Biographical Frame

Although I hoped to wake at seven a.m., this morning I
woke at five thirty. The world is made of surprises, I
Belted out to cheer myself up, calling to my dear dog for a
walk. Biscuit was in his doghouse sleeping
Comfy on his foam rubber bed. Before sunrise and before
everyone wakes up is a good time to walk a
Dog. Biscuit did take a dump in a neighbor's yard. It was
too dark and wet to risk a shotgun blast
Exiting energetically a Texas neighbor's window by slipping
into his yard to pick up the poop in a
Flimsy plastic bag. The dog and I sloshed through big rain
puddles, he in his bare feet, I in my sandals.
Grasped a black umbrella with one broken spoke. The rain
spoke the beat to me from the umbrella like a
Hot jazz drummer playing a complex rhythm with a lot of
pauses. A few cars went by up at the corner
Interestingly sounding like hamburgers sizzling on a grill.
Here it's October seventeenth and still warm enough.
Just to go ahead and get out in the crazy rain of morning in
a t-shirt with a gecko on it, shorts, plus your
K-Mart hippie sandals. We needed the rain. Where I live,
we always need the rain. We don't have soil,
Lots of white sand we have, left over when the Gulf of
Mexico reached this far inland. Down the street
Most of the needles on one pine in a small grove have turned
a lovely shade of brown and the tree has
Now died, yet each day's a miracle. Watching plants survive,
and, in certain seasons, even thrive is
Obviously an immense gift and grace from the Mystery. We
get drinking water from wells and
Plentifully we humans thrive. How did the water get way

175

down deep inside the rock? At 113 degrees it's
Quite hot so it must be cooled down by tall water-cooling
   towers. The water's high in sodium so it's
Rough on some plants and a lot of the humans filter it to
   make it go down easier. I have three kids, one
Still at home, my daughter Bev, and two boys grown and
   on their own, Bill and Brent are fully living
Their lives in a place of limestone rock, lakes, caves, and
   black land prairie; they're blessed by and
Under the influence of this amazing place chocked full of
   cultural variety—black, brown, white—
Very creative people in science and the arts. Thanksgiving's
   coming and I think it was a wonderful
Wise spiritual leader on Oprah who said the best prayer
   you can give is to say "Thanks." Get paper and
Xerox off the simple phrase "Thank You" and pass it out
   on sheets at corners to the elderly and the
Young walking by, and I hope where you are now on the
   streets walking your dog the temperature is not
Zero and you're not wading through drifts, yet saying
   thanks, loving the pee stains sunk in the snow.

abcdefghijklmnopqrstuvwxyz

Thank you!

9 781936 671175